SHAME
A SECRETS AND LIES NOVEL

AINSLEY BOOTH

ABOUT THIS BOOK

Grace:
I never thought my husband would cheat on me. I was wrong.
Now I need to pick up the tattered remnants of my life and
figure out how to put one foot in front of the other. How to
look at myself in the mirror without seeing my own secrets
scrawled there in shameful scarlet.

Luke:
I am exactly the asshole you think I am.
I don't deserve her. I should walk away. But I can't let her go
without a fight. Too late—too damn late—I'm realizing what
I've done and everything that I've lost.
Everything I want back again, or maybe really to have and to
hold properly for the first time. In order to stay with Grace
and win her back, I'm going to need to storm through fire,
over and over again.

You can't help who you love

If you want to leave him, leave him. Be happy. You deserve that. But if you are tied to him inextricably—for your own reasons, not his, never his—then take this to heart. You have a right to be happy. You have a right to break him, as he has broken you, and maybe from the ashes something new and good will come. On your terms, you beautiful goddess. Forever. And he can take it or leave it. You have all the power now. Use it wisely. Use it for yourself. Use it for the truth.

GRACE

I NEVER THOUGHT my husband would cheat on me.

I was sure of it.

I was wrong.

Luke: Are you going to be home for dinner?

Grace: Should be.

Luke: I'll pick something up.

Grace: No red meat!

Luke: I know. Love you!

Grace: Love you, too.

"I'M HOPPING in the shower. I gotta head out for a bit."

"Where are you going?"

"I told you, I have a thing."

I frown. I don't remember him mentioning an event. "Is it something you need me for?"

"Nope. Just a meeting. I won't be long, but don't wait up."

I never do. As I've moved into my thirties, I've decided I like going to sleep early and waking up early to get a workout in before I start my day.

Luke, on the other hand, is a confirmed night owl.

When we were first married, we'd stay up late together, until I got sleepy, and then he'd tuck me into bed and read beside me while I fell asleep. I don't remember the last time he did that, but really, if he did, I'd just get annoyed, because then I wouldn't be able to read something dirty and get myself off.

A quick, efficient orgasm is better than any sleeping pill ever invented. And while I love sex with Luke, there is no such thing as a quick orgasm with him. And lately, sometimes there's no orgasm at all.

When the stars align, though, sex is fantastic. It still takes a while, though. Luke has a rule—I always come first, and preferably twice. You'd think this would be a great rule. It's the stuff of internet memes. But it's actually more pressure than I want, and he won't be dissuaded of it. *Just fucking use my body as a receptacle for your come* is not something my husband will ever understand.

Nor is it something I could ever say with a straight face. Not without bursting into flames. This is on my mind as he moves towards the en suite bathroom adjacent to our bedroom. I catch his hand and tug him close, wanting his bulk against me. He kisses me softly and brushes past instead. No bulk. No hot kiss.

I sigh at his retreating back, but he doesn't notice.

He disappears into the bathroom, and I turn around again, catching sight of his phone on the bed. "Hey, baby, you forgot your—"

But the shower's already on.

The screen lights up. There's a text message notification on the screen.

Spitfire

Text Message

Spitfire. Who the hell would be in his phone book as *Spitfire?* My pulse starts to pound as I starc at the screen. The locked screen.

IIe has a thing tonight?

And a text message from someone named Spitfire?

Fingers shaking, I tap the home button. The password screen slides into view. Fucking hell, I don't know what it is.

On a whim, I try his bank card pin code. That's what I use, and we're so alike...

It works.

From a distance, I feel myself smiling, but it feels wrong, because I know what I'm about to find.

Somehow, deep down inside, I know exactly what Spitfire is. I don't know who she is, but I know she's my husband's lover.

And I know my heart is about to break.

2

LUKE

My back is tight, and the hot water isn't helping. I should cancel drinks with Caitlyn tonight.

I won't, though.

Rolling my neck, I scrub soap over my chest and down my belly.

I need to go back to the fucking gym.

I need to stop eating McDonald's.

I need to do a lot of fucking things, but I won't, and I don't.

Dark, ugly thoughts crowd the back of my mind, and I turn the temperature of the shower down. Cold, sharp drops hit my skin.

That's good. Sharp, intense.

A lot like Caitlyn.

My dick twitches, and I will it to work tonight. *Hold her down, fuck her mouth until she gags.* Yeah, that would feel amazing.

I turn the shower off and reach for the towel I put on the hook just outside the walk-in shower.

It's not there.

"Grace," I holler out, ignoring the way my stomach twists.

I've gotten good at shoving that weird twinge away.

She doesn't respond, so I walk around the corner, water sluicing off me. Maybe I left it on the—

But I didn't.

My towel is in Grace's hand. She's perched on the vanity, a little bird, clutching the towel. And my phone.

Her face is white.

"Who is Spitfire?" she asks, her voice barely a whisper.

My heart stops.

The pain on her face surprises me. I don't know why. I've been cheating on her and she's just found out.

I put that pain there.

But that realization is like an out-of-body thought, totally disjointed from the desperate, clawing question hurtling around inside my head.

What have I done? What I have done to my wife?

My wife.

Grace.

"I can explain," I say dumbly, because I don't need to. She knows.

"Who. Is.—"

I reach my hand out. "Give me my phone."

She shakes her head. "Nope. I've already sent myself every-thing, anyway."

There isn't much there. I'm diligent about deleting the

content regularly. But I still... My brain screams at me to get this under control.

"What's her name?"

"It doesn't matter." My skin crawls at the thought of Grace knowing anything about...

I can't even think her name again.

That woman.

My mistake.

"Are you for real?" Grace chucks my phone at me and I barely catch it. "Are you for fucking real? Trying to protect this woman? I will find her, you pig. I have her phone number."

She hops off the vanity and spins away, a whirlwind of righteous anger.

And I'm standing there, holding my phone, naked. Still dripping wet from the shower.

I chase her anyway. "Wait."

She laughs and grabs something off her dresser, whipping it in my general direction. "Fuck off."

"I'm not trying to protect her. She's meaningless. A mistake."

"Those texts don't look like mistakes. They look deliberate. They look like a choice you made."

"I..." I wipe my hand over my face. "I need to get dressed."

She gestures at my dresser. "Help yourself. Empty all the drawers while you're at it, because I want you out of here tonight."

"We need to talk."

"Who is she?"

My heart is pounding in my chest as I pull on a t-shirt and a pair of sweatpants.

She snorts. "Fine. I'll call her Spitfire, then. *Dear Spitfire, my husband won't be making drinks with you tonight. Or ever again.*"

I groan as she types out a text message.

There's no way Cait will reply.

She knows better.

I hope so, anyway.

God. Fucking. Damn. "You don't need to do that. I'm happy to stay home tonight."

She laughs again. "Home?" She waves around. "This place where we have occasional, simple sex? Where you mostly dodge me and wait until I'm asleep before you crawl into bed?"

My gut turns over and my skin goes cold at the accurate barb. "Yes, home."

"Who. Is. She?"

I give her a little. "She's an outside counsel we used once at the firm."

"Someone you work with."

"Worked with once."

"I see."

"I love you."

She laughs hysterically. "No, you don't."

"I do. Please, let me—"

Holding up her hand, she shakes her head. "Nah. Don't bother. I'm going to leave."

"Don't leave." Desperate need storms inside me. I'll say

anything to keep her here. "I know this is awful. I know you have questions. I know—"

"How long have you been in a relationship with someone else?"

"It's not like that." It's honest to God not. How can I make her see that? "I swear to you, it's over. Done. I don't care about that woman. I never did."

That's the truth. At least part of it.

She hesitates. It's a glimmer of hope, and I latch on to it with every bit of my vicious, Bay Street-honed training. I know when a negotiation turns my way, and this one—as fucked up as that is, and I own that—just broke for the bad guys.

Fucking hell.

I swallow hard. "She's nothing, Grace. You are everything. Whatever you need. Whatever you want. I love you. Please, give me a chance to fix this."

3

GRACE

I scream at him for hours. Throw things at him. He refuses to leave, and eventually, at dawn, I fall asleep on the couch. I wake up an hour later, jolted awake by dark, gross nightmares.

He's curled up on the floor beside me, his hand up on the couch right next to my hand. Not touching me, but close enough that I can feel the heat of his skin.

I should recoil. I *want* to recoil. But I need his warmth more. I nudge the edge of my hand against his, and he lets out a shuddering groan, then wraps his fingers around mine. "I know I've fucked up."

His voice is raw, his eyes red.

I sit up and look at him. He's rumpled. Ashen-faced and needs a shave. He looks…old. And broken.

Get out, I say in my head. It doesn't translate to words out loud, though.

"I can't sleep," I whisper, and he pulls me into his chest.

"I know. I'm sorry."

"I hate you."

"Yeah. Me too."

The tears come again, and he holds me tight as I soak the front of his t-shirt. Eventually I fall asleep again, exhausted, and when I wake up for the second time, it's mid-morning.

Luke is passed out beneath me on the couch.

We're both damp with sweat and my heart is pounding.

I roll onto my back and press the heel of my hand to my forehead. God. When was the last time Luke slept in this late? He'll be pissed.

And then right on the heels of that thought is another, more bitter one. Why do I care? His schedule is not my problem. His work is not my problem.

Fuck.

I kick at the blanket he pulled over us.

"What's wrong?" he mumbles.

I don't say anything. I just keep wrestling with the throw until I'm free, then I lurch to my feet. I stumble to the kitchen and go through the motions of making coffee.

Luke follows. A big shadow of a man. He doesn't any anything at first. The silence looms, ugly and familiar. He never says much.

We don't talk anymore.

And when he does open his mouth, it's the inevitable retreat. His evergreen excuse to get away from me. "I have to go to work for a few hours."

Work. I slam the cupboard door shut. "Where you fucked her."

"I never— Never at the office. It wasn't like that. It was stupid and private."

Things like that are never as private as people think. "Who knows about the affair?"

"Nobody."

"Sam wouldn't cover it up. He'd have told me. Does your assistant know?"

"No."

"Are you sure?" There's an unstable edge to my voice and I hate it. I'm not out of control here, he is. I'm just asking questions I have every right to know the answer to. "Why do you have to go to work, anyway? Are you going to destroy more evidence?"

"I'm going to take some time off. It'll be easier to explain that in person. I need to pick up a few things. Bring a laptop home."

I spin around. "You're the fucking boss, Luke. Have them courier you your shit." But then another thought forms in my head. If he leaves for a bit, I can search his closet. I sigh and square my shoulders. Easier to be the bigger person when you're secretly a petty, vindictive bitch. "Okay. No, I get it. Go to work."

"I won't be long."

"I might change the locks while you're gone."

His nostrils flare. "Don't do that. I'm going to get some stuff so I can work from home for a few weeks. We're going to get through this."

The only thing I'm going to get through is a divorce, and I'm going to do it like a fucking winner. In the cold light of day, I've moved into an icy calm. Yelling at him didn't work. Now I need to get strategic.

THAT RESOLVE to be smart and strategic lasts an hour. I don't find anything in his belongings, no secret love letters or obvious receipts that spell out the extent of his betrayal.

The silence of the apartment is suffocating, and the size of all that I don't know about my husband's affair looms large, filling the space.

Pressing against my skin.

You're an idiot. A sucker. A fool.

I look at my phone, at the screenshots I texted myself before I confronted Luke.

A terrible need drives me to keep looking at them. Afraid of what I will find. Desperate to find it all the same.

And then I go to my computer. I put her phone number into the search engine and get nothing, but when I go to Facebook and paste it there, voila.

A profile image.

A name.

Caitlyn Jobst. A junior lawyer. Younger than me by the looks of it, because of course she is.

She's beautiful. Lush and sexy, pouring out of dresses on the arms of handsome men. Every picture is almost exactly the same, like she knows the right angle to always look at the camera. Pettily I wonder if she hates being photographed from the other side, if she has a wonky smile or a double chin, but that's not likely.

I can see why he was drawn to her. She looks just like the women in the porn he likes. Big boobs.

Have you ever thought about getting implants? I think of all the times his hands have covered my breasts and squeezed. Barely a handful, one bigger than the other. I'd always brush off the question, because no, seriously, never, but was that his way of saying he wanted me bigger?

Did he want me to look like her? Dark hair, flashing eyes, perfect makeup? Plumped up and pushed up in every way possible? Soft skin, no dry elbows, no scattering of prickle rash down the back of her arms?

No doughy middle, no pear-shaped hips with too much thigh and not enough length through the calves.

Of course he fucked her.

Of course he wanted that.

I went from being strategic and looking for information to arm myself to just hurting myself for no good fucking reason.

The tears fall again, fast and furious, and I shove the computer away. I want to crawl into a hole and die.

4

LUKE

COLD, slick fear rolls through me as I force myself onto the elevator at my office. There's a solid chance Grace won't be home when I return, or she'll have changed the locks.

My hands shake as I push the buttons, my head swimming with details I usually catalogue with cold efficiency. I need to buy myself some time. I need to repair the damage I've done and make some urgent changes.

When I arrive at our firm's floor, I nod curtly to the receptionist, then head straight to my office. My assistant Cameron isn't at his desk, which is for the best. I don't want my messages first thing. I hear his voice filtering from down the hall, coming closer, so I quickly open my door and duck inside, then lock the door and close the blinds.

Fuck.

I slam my eyelids shut and press my back against the door.

This is embarrassing.

14

You own the fucking firm, you dipshit. Just tell them you're taking a week off. You don't need to explain yourself to anyone.

Except I do.

My father's voice echoes in my head, dripping with condescension. *"How did you not notice what he was doing? How did you let this happen under your nose?"*

Never once did he think I'd known about Sam's reckless behaviour and let it slide. He'd gone straight to incompetence.

Would he judge me in the same way for destroying my marriage?

They had never liked Grace much. The dislike was mutual.

Not that he liked his own wife, either.

Was infidelity and marital cruelty hereditary?

In front of me, my monitor blinks on. Our internal messaging system pops up. Cameron is back at his desk and has noticed I'm here.

Great. Don't mind me, I'm just having a meltdown.

I move to the desk, shoving thoughts of my parents back into the dark, gross hole where I usually keep them.

Cameron: Messages are on your desk. Let me know when you have a free minute to go over meeting requests for the week.

He's been with me for almost two years, the longest any assistant has lasted at that desk, and he's used to me being a bear.

I start to type back some excuse, but it's a lie even as much as it's the truth.

The real truth is, I need him to lie for me.

Can I trust you, Cameron? Well, I'm not going that far. I'm not a fucking idiot.

I stalk back to the door and yank it open. "Come in."

His expression doesn't change as he takes in my appearance—unshaved, no suit. Look of death pasted on my face.

Who died?

Me, if I have anything to say about it.

As soon as the door closes behind him, I open my mouth to tell him I need him to cover for me—and nothing comes out.

He frowns.

I turn to the window and take a deep breath. Then I pivot back and pick up the messages. One thing at a time.

The name on the second piece of paper curdles the blood in my veins.

She doesn't call me here. Ever. My fingers shake as I keep flipping, then go back to the first one. "Georgian Bay VC cancelled our meeting?"

He nods.

I shrug. "Okay."

Flip. My fingers tighten. "Caitlyn Jobst called?"

"She didn't say what it was about."

"Okay." Another flip. I read the name on the third slip of paper. I don't care. We don't always go through them, but I just needed to know she hadn't said anything else.

Do not fucking call me at the office.

"Do you want to go over the meeting requests for next week?"

"Yep." *Do not call—* "No." I clear my throat. "I need to take some time away from the office."

Now it's his turn to say okay. He doesn't ask why.

I swallow hard. *I need you to tell my brother.* "I don't want to tell anyone just yet."

"Understood."

Ask me why. Make me say it. "I'll be accessible on my phone and I'll take my laptop home."

"Sure."

"Alex can take any venture capitalist meetings we can't move."

He nods. "You spoke to him already?"

The way he looks at the door, I realize my friend is in the building.

Did I tell him that I broke Grace's heart? Fuck no. "He's here." It comes out like a flat statement. Does Cameron interpret that as a positive answer to his question? "I haven't spoken to him yet. Can you tell him I need to see him."

Another flat statement. I haven't been able to ask a single question properly since *Caitlyn Jobst called?*

I'm broken.

I've broken both of us.

"Give me five minutes to return these messages, first. Then tell him I need to see him."

Cameron leaves, closing the door behind him.

I'm alone with the messages, and I dig for a lighter in my bottom drawer. Next to the pack of smokes I keep for when someone needs to go up to the roof and have a Come to Jesus moment about taking their business public.

I burn the message, watch her name curl into dust.

Then I open an incognito browser, go to a web email account I will delete as soon as I send one final message, and I email my former lover a short, curt note telling her we have nothing to talk about. We both knew the deal. What we had was disposable—we just both assumed it would be her who disposed of me when I stopped being useful to her.

```
We can't speak again. What we did was a
terrible mistake and I regret hurting
my wife.
```

Even as I type that, my fingers clench against the keyboard. I don't want to bring Grace up here. I never wanted those two parts of my life to exist in the same space.

I was a fool.

A red haze blurs my vision as I try to figure out how to delete the stupid account. I close it, telling myself I'll do it after I talk to Alex.

Then I close my computer only for my gaze to fall on my leather journal, where I keep a cryptic record of everything in my life.

Including my affair, sometimes.

Yesterday, I'd scribbled down the time and her initials. I rip that page out and light it on fire, too, watching it burn. I repeat that for a few other pages I can find.

It occurs to me I should burn the whole thing, but that size of a fire might set off the sprinklers and someone might report my erratic behaviour to the exchange commission.

Just what we need. Another Preston meltdown to send the Bay Street whisper network into top gear.

Fuck, what a mess.

A knock at the door is followed by it swinging open. Only one person isn't afraid of what will happen when they stroll into my office uninvited—a man who is closer to me than my own brother, better than me by half, and smart enough to have walked away from this life before it ate it him alive.

Alex sniffs as he settles casually into the chair across from my desk. He's wearing jeans and a blazer, with a leather messenger bag strapped across his body. He looks more like a hip marketing executive than the business shark he once had been—or the elusive writer he had since become. "Do you smell smoke?"

"I burned a note."

He gives me a weird look, because that's a weird fucking thing to do. "Cameron paged me."

"He mentioned you were in the building. This is a nice surprise."

He shrugs. "I was looking for Sam."

Alex and I go back to business school. He was my friend first, but he's closer to my brother now. Just like Grace, just like everyone. "He's not here. He's working at his girlfriend's house outside the city this week."

"Hazel's great, isn't she?" There's a challenge in Alex's eyes.

I nod. Is she? I should know that. Grace probably likes her. I don't think we've exchanged five words. "You looking for Sam, was that business or something personal?"

"Somewhere in between." He doesn't elaborate. They've cut me out of a lot of things over the past two years.

I haven't been pleasant to be around.

He stretches his arms wide, his blazer falling open to reveal a *Headstones* band t-shirt. "What did you want?"

"I'm taking a leave of absence. Quietly. Sam doesn't know."

Alex's eyebrows hit the roof. "Everything okay?"

No. "Yeah. I just need a break. I'm wondering if you might be able to field the venture capitalist meetings for a week or two."

When we graduated business school, we both came to Bay Street. I started as a trader at my father's firm. Alex went into consulting, rising rapidly through the ranks because he had a knack for efficiency and delivering bad news with a smile.

When Sam was arrested, he left consulting and came on board as a trustee here. It was supposed to be for a year, until I could prove to the regulators we were on the up and up. And then he surprised the shit out of us by wanting to stay on, part time, because the fucker had gone and written a kids' book.

He's now an author most of the time, who sometimes roams the halls here and makes brilliant investments in companies he likes.

"I can clear my calendar," he says easily. "Can I use your assistant while you're away?"

"I'm not going anywhere," I snap. "I'll be at home. It's a ten-minute drive."

He gives me a bland, *your bark doesn't scare me* look. "So that's a yes, Cameron is mine while you decompress?"

"Sure."

"Is this about Grace's show?"

I frown.

Alex groans. "It's in two weeks, Luke, don't tell me you don't know about it. She's really excited."

I know about it. A new wave of sick feelings twist inside me. "It's not about her show," I grind out.

His neutral expression drops, revealing an uncharacteristic slice of raw anger. "Good. Because Sam told me you weren't happy about it."

5

GRACE

Six weeks earlier

I WENT from elated to deflated in the span of a short phone call with my husband, so I'm going to Sam's to share my news with someone who actually cares about my career.

He's on the phone with his girlfriend Hazel when I arrive and he waves me in.

I've brought food, so I head to the kitchen, and as I set the takeout on the counter, something catches my eye. A VIP card for The Wheelhouse. *Sam?* Dirty boy.

He's right behind me, telling Hazel he has to go, as I hold up the card.

He groans. "Yep, totally fine. It's just Grace nosing in my private business. Give me five minutes to kick her out and then I'm all yours again."

I laugh at him. "You didn't need to end the call on my account."

He glowers. "What are you doing here?"

"Feeding you."

"I have food."

Ouch. "Feeding myself in your presence because Luke is working late, and I was lonely, then."

"Ah." But he looks at his phone, and I realize belatedly that I'm not welcome right now. Crap.

I should go. I don't, because I'm feeling small and sad inside. I put on a brave face. "Call her back. I don't care if you're busy, I just like the hum of another person in my space."

Then I look down at the card. Maybe if we both laugh about it... "The Wheelhouse, eh? I wouldn't have pegged you for the type."

"You can't do this," he bursts out.

I drop the card on the counter.

"I know you mean well, and I love you for it, but...I was talking to my girlfriend. That card...is because I want to *go there* with my girlfriend. You can't just waltz into my house and make this awkward for me!"

Fuck. Fuck. I'm shaking as I nod. "Of course."

"Grace..."

"No, I get it. I'll take my food and go to the studio instead. There are usually people there all night."

He makes a face. "I've gone about this poorly."

"Probably," I whisper. "But is there a right way to remind someone they're tromping on boundaries? Maybe not. It's fine. I'll go, and I'll text next time I'm looking for dinner company."

I grab the food and head for the door, my pulse pounding loud in my ears.

I'm an idiot. If Sam wants to go to a kink club, that's his personal business. Most people don't have the same openness around sex that I do—hell, Luke doesn't, of course his brother wouldn't.

The elevator comes quickly, and I keep my head down as I sweep across the lobby of his building.

I'm nearly to my car when I hear Sam shout behind me.

I stop and turn back.

He jogs to a stop in front of me. "I'm sorry, I reacted badly. Do you want to come back upstairs? Or do you want company at the studio?"

There's something in the way he says it, like I could maybe ask him for anything, that I try again, my second attempt to impress a Preston man today. "Actually, I want to show you something. If you're game?"

And because he's awesome, he gives me a broad grin and tells me to take him anywhere I want to go—which is an art gallery on the edge of the fashion district.

The parking spot right in front is free, so I slide into it. Then I swallow around the sharp bundle of nerves in my throat and tell him my news.

"I'm going to have a show here next month. I told Luke about it today, and he said, and I quote, 'As long as my name isn't attached to it.' Can you believe him?"

Sam makes a face like, yes, he totally can believe that about his brother. "I'm sorry."

"Yeah. Me, too." I turn the car off. "Come on. I have a key."

I lead him through the current exhibit to a door, which leads to a back room. This is the staging area for our show, which will be installed in a few weeks. Sam looks around, taking in the mishmash of work. My sculptures, some metalwork designs, and some paintings, too.

"This is…a joint show? Next month?" Sam asks.

I nod. "Alex put me in touch with a local patron, who was already helping the other two artists get this show off the ground. When Alex mentioned that I used to work in the gallery world, and might have a few pieces I could contribute, I…well, I jumped into the deep end. I didn't know I wanted this. I thought my online business was enough, but there's nothing quite like a show, Sam. I'm…"

"And then Luke shit all over it."

"Yeah."

"And then I yelled at you for interrupting my phone date."

That sums it up. "Yes. But I think you were more embarrassed that I saw the VIP night card, right?"

He blushes. "Yeah, probably."

"That's why I wanted to show you this. It's Deke—the owner—who Alex wanted me to meet. So if you have the VIP card, you should know that you might see my work at his club. And…you might see me, there, too."

He stares at me, agape.

Well, cat's out of the bag now.

"That's a secret," I say tightly. "From your brother, too."

"Grace…"

"I'm not doing anything wrong." I can't look at him, because while I know that's true by the letter of the law, I'm not sure it's true in spirit. *Whatever. Luke isn't open with me about shit fuck all.* "I just didn't want you to be surprised. That's all."

"I don't know what to say."

"You don't need to say anything. Just hear it, and then... you know, in time."

He clears his throat. "I'm proud of you. I know that much."

"Thanks."

"And I'm starving. Can we eat?"

"Of course." I tug a canvas drop cloth off my newest sculpture and set it on the ground. "Do you mind having a picnic on the floor?"

"No." He's looking at the piece. "Is this yours?"

Maybe it was the wrong one to grab a drop cloth from, but he'll see it at the show. "Yeah."

"It's not a woman."

"I branch out sometimes."

It's a man, head ducked low. No face visible, because his heavy body is twisted away, and a woman's arms are embracing him. Would Sam recognize his brother's back? My hands? Maybe it's for the best that Luke wants nothing to do with a show I'm putting on where my centre piece is called *Death of a Marriage.*

6

LUKE

Present day

Fuck. Grace's *show*. Not that there is ever a good time to discover your husband is a bastard, but two weeks before a huge career shift... I swallow hard and glower at Alex. "I don't know what Sam told you, but it sounds like none of your business."

"I'm trying to help Grace here," he grinds out.

Alex never gets mad. Maybe I shouldn't have asked him to cover for me. "Listen," I say, my heart hammering as I lean in. "I appreciate that. I know I haven't been as understanding as I could be about her art, but if I blew her off in the past, it was a mistake."

One of many.

My friend shakes his head. "Well, that's for you to make up to her. I can't imagine it will be easy."

He has no fucking idea.

I clear my throat. "Do you have the details about the show?"

He rolls his eyes and pulls a glossy booklet out of his bag. It has the name of a gallery on the front, then a set of dates, and three names. *Grace Dunn* is listed in the middle.

I'd barked at her that I didn't want my name associated with her art. But it never had been. She always created under her maiden name. She didn't use Preston for anything anymore. There had been a time when that had been her name, her identity. In the early days of this firm, she'd played the role of the corporate wife to perfection.

She'd hated it.

She'd already taken up art when our firm collapsed. When our assets were seized, she pivoted her hobby into a career, leveraging whatever connections she could to springboard her catalogue into online infamy.

Other people—my parents, for example—would have died of shame to have their work mocked by Buzzfeed. Grace *orchestrated* that, and raked in enough private commissions of erotic sculpture from the visibility to buy our new home.

A loft where she brought my fuck-up of a brother to lick his wounds.

Alex leaves me alone with the booklet and a pile of regret he can't even begin to understand.

I pack everything I might need to deal with an emergency from home and head out, not saying goodbye to anyone as I leave.

Echos of bad decisions chase me down the elevator and into my car.

I never thought I would have to look at my mistakes quite so squarely in the face. I never liked what I was doing—except when I did, briefly, because I'm a base animal inside. I lived with gross regret on a daily basis, but never did anything about it.

Even the inside of my car reminds me of driving to hotels, sending furtive texts on arrival. Ruining everything, over and over again.

The conversation I had with Grace about her show reverberates in my head. That was a day I'd gone out and fucked around on her. Got my hit of illicit feel good, feel bad vibes and took out my guilt on her excitement.

I need to talk to her about the show, too. And the weight of all the ways I've fucked up make it impossible to get out of my car. When I arrive at home, I sit in my parking spot for far too long.

I don't want to go upstairs. I don't want to see Grace's sad face.

You can walk away.

She would be happier if I did, in the long run. Get out of her way and let her heal. Watch her move on.

I should leave her. But the thought of it fills me with terror. I need Grace for reasons I've never needed to spell out before, can't even now as I sit in the underground garage and try to pull the words to my tongue.

I just need her. And I forgot, maybe, or lost sight of how much.

Taking a deep breath, I grab my bag. The elevator from the garage level that would take me to the back of the loft is out of order, so I take the stairs to the lobby, then take the main elevator up to our floor. There are four lofts per floor. One of them has a private elevator to the garage, although it's been on the fritz for months. We are that loft on our floor.

Grace chose it for me. The loft is all her, but the private elevator that goes to the parking garage—that was a luxury she chose for me.

And I fucking hate that it doesn't work. I hate that I share it with the other ten loft owners who stack above and below us.

I miss my Forest Hill mansion.

I *lost* that house, along with everything else.

Me. I. Me. My.

I resented how Grace barely tripped over my life imploding. She kept going, pulled us back up, and I watched her surpass me in every way. And I let that resentment fester.

When we met, I was the rock she leaned on, a stable force for a whirlwind young woman who had come from an unstable background.

Once upon a time, the monumental amount of chaos she carries in her small frame excited me. When we met, she seemed hedonistic and wonderful, perfect and erotic.

We were complete opposites, and the attraction had been instantaneous. Lasting.

And then Sam ruined everything.

It was ruined before that.

Where the fuck was this second-guessing voice in my head six months ago? A year ago?

Drugged. Drowned in scotch and smothered by easy escape.

The collapse of our firm revealed me to myself as weak in a shocking and pathetic way. I wasn't able to share anything but the briefest of updates with Grace. I found myself lying to her, hiding things, terrified she would blame me for bringing this ruin upon us.

And once I was lying to her about money and business, it was easy to lean into lies in other ways. Private ways.

I realize with a start that I'm now standing in front of our front door. I let myself in to a dangerously quiet space.

"Grace," I call out, my voice shaking. "I'm back."

No reply. Dropping my bag, I head straight to the bedroom, prepared to see her closet empty and suitcases gone.

Instead, I find her asleep on the bed, her face blotchy.

7

GRACE

I DRIFT AWAKE, half-conscious when I realize Luke is wrapped around me, spooning me from behind.

His arm is heavy around my waist. His palm pressed to my belly. His thighs, longer than mine, are wedged right against my legs.

And for a moment, I'm struck with a deep familiarity. It's been too long, but once upon a time, he would hold me like this all the time.

If I wake all the way up, I'll push him away and jump out of bed. I *am* going to do that very soon, in fact. But he's so warm and I can feel his heartbeat.

Don't cry. I've cried enough today, and felt so lonely I wanted to crawl out of my skin. I must have passed out on the bed while he was at work, and now he's here, holding me.

Warm.

Strong.

Cheater.

I start to shake, and he makes a soothing sound from behind me. "I'm here," he says, tightening his arms around me. His voice is rough, like gravel. "Is this okay?"

No. But I nod, because I like it even as I hate it.

"I'm sorry I went to the office." He buries his face in my hair. "I shouldn't have left you. We have so much to talk about."

"I don't want to talk," I whisper. My voice is gravelly, too. "I need to…" I trail off. It doesn't matter. Not today.

"Do you have work to do for your show?"

Tears spill out from behind my eyelids and fall in wet, fat drops on my pillow. "You're not interested in that, remember?"

He swears under his breath. "I remember. I'm sorry."

And we're done cuddling. I push myself up, and he rolls onto his back, his arm falling over his face.

I go to the closet and find myself some clean clothes, then go into the bathroom where just last night I confronted him about the affair. Was that less than twenty-four hours ago? I lock the door and start the shower.

I TAKE my time when I'm done, drying my hair and carefully applying serums to my face because I'm not fresh out of law school. Then I get dressed before opening the door to the bedroom again.

Luke is sitting on the bed. He looks like he's been run over by a truck.

Good.

He straightens up and gives me a desperate look. "Are you hungry?"

I shake my head.

"Let me cook something for dinner."

I don't want him to do anything nice for me right now. "We can order in."

"I want—"

"I couldn't fucking care less what you want." I pin him with a sharp glare, meant to hurt.

He holds the gaze like an eager puppy, like any attention is good attention, which is probably what got him into this situation in the first place.

Pathetic.

He shrugs. "Fair enough. We'll order in whatever you want. Maybe that's better. Give us more time to talk—"

"I don't want to talk," I mutter.

Luke keeps going. "I want to give you my full attention. Fix what I've broken. You have a show coming up—"

"I don't want to talk," I repeat louder this time. "Because of the show. Because I'm a mess inside." My voice raises. "Because I can't look at you without shaking."

And because I already miss the warmth of his body wrapped around me.

I hate you, I think in my head.

"Don't look at me, then." He gets up and moves to the armchair by the fireplace, out of my direct line of sight.

I move to the spot on the bed he just vacated, grab the

blanket, and wrap that lingering residual heat around my body.

I'm hollow inside.

I want him to hold me again.

I hate him.

I curl onto my side and stare out the window at the sky.

Luke clears his throat. "I saw Alex at the office. Just him and Cameron, that was it. I told them I need to quietly take some time and work from home. Alex is going to cover my meetings —and he gave me shit for not being supportive of your show."

"That's why you asked about it."

"He reminded me I'd been a dick to you. I'm sorry."

I don't reply to that. It's hardly the most important problem in front of us right now. But now that he's brought it up, my mind races with the to-do list I have for the next two weeks.

And then the opening night itself. I'm certainly not looking forward to pasting on a smile that will hurt by the end of three hours, pressing flesh with potential buyers for a catalogue of work that in an instant, my husband blew up my entire practiced pitch for.

The *Death in a Marriage* piece certainly takes on a new meaning. But all the other pieces are just as deadly to me. Each of them represents in a subtle way the erotic fantasies I had about Luke.

I'm a fool.

A fool who is going to have to sell pieces that no longer feel real to me.

Fuck.

Throwing off the blanket, I force myself to stand. "I need to go to the studio." I swallow hard. "I might stay there tonight. I need some space."

Luke's out of the chair before I get to the bedroom door. He gets in front of me, blocking the exit, and I see red. I shove at his chest and burst into tears.

"Go to Sam's," he mutters under his breath. "He's at Hazel's for the week. Don't sleep at the studio."

I shove again and he bumps against the door frame, then slides out of the way.

I don't look back. I grab my bag and my coat and leave before the tears consume me.

8

LUKE

I SPEND a sleepless night alone in our bed. I can't get warm, even wearing a sweater. At some point in the middle of the night, I pull on a hoodie from college that Grace had long ago appropriated as hers.

It smells like her.

And as I stare at the clock turn to half-past three in the morning, something inside me cracks. I reach for my phone in the dark and it lights up as I pick it up.

Grace: I can't sleep. I hate you. I just thought you should know.

Luke: I can't sleep either. I love you. And I understand.

Grace: I hate my show, too.

Luke: Can we talk? Can you call me?

She doesn't reply, and the phone doesn't ring. After a long, painful minute that feels like an hour, I try her phone, but it doesn't go through.

Dawn comes before I fall asleep. I wake up with a start not long after, thinking I feel the weight of her sliding into bed next to me. But the loft is still empty.

9

GRACE

IT WAS a mistake to text him. I block him right after he says he loves me—*no you don't, you don't know what that word means*—and then I spend an hour watching and reading porn, trying to get myself off so the post-orgasm release will trip me into sleep.

It's fucking rude that Luke's affair has ruined some of my favourite smut subjects, too.

There's no point raiding Sam's cupboards for booze, either, because he doesn't have anything. I find a single serving bottle of cheap champagne that's covered in dust and undrinkable when I open it.

I hope he never wonders where that bottle went, because tomorrow I'll find a better place to stay. I can't stay here much longer without him figuring out I'm here, and...I'm not ready for that. As it stands, I'm already a creeper for letting myself in without telling him I'm there.

On the other hand, I know this apartment like the back of

my hand. I helped Sam buy it, desperate to get him out of our place.

I thought Luke and I would be able to get back on track once we had our private life back.

I was wrong.

After pouring the bad sparkling wine down the drain, I steal a cheese stick from the fridge and go back to bed.

My second attempt at a desperate orgasm-to-sleep strategy works better.

When I wake up, it's mid-morning, and my phone tells me it's time to go back to the studio.

I made a long to-do list yesterday. I hate every single item on the list, don't want to do any of it, but I'm a professional.

It's time to get shit done for Future Grace, who will be very upset at me for making life even more difficult for her down the road if I don't pull myself out of this pity party.

After putting my bedding in the washing machine, I make Sam's spare bed with fresh sheets and go out to get a late breakfast.

When I walk past my car, parked on the street, I do a double-take because Luke is parked behind me. He's slumped behind the steering wheel, wearing an old hoodie from university.

He looks like a stalker.

He's acting like a stalker.

I throw my hands in the air and glare at him as he gets out of the car. "What are you doing here?"

"You blocked my number."

"I didn't want to talk to you."

"You texted me."

"A mistake."

"I just wanted to see if you were…" He trails off.

I'm not okay. I wrap my arms around myself and shiver.

"Are you going to the studio?"

"Yes." Eventually.

He glances at my car.

I could get in, but then I'd lose my prime spot, and I need to come back and put the sheets in the dryer after breakfast.

"After I get some food," I mumble.

He turns and looks down the street, toward the hub of restaurants and shops not far from Sam's place. "Can I join you?"

"No."

His face falls.

Walk away.

But all I see is the sad, lonely boy in the cafeteria at dawn, studying his ass off.

No pity.

I wish I was smart enough to take my own inner advice. I sigh. "You know what? Sure. You can buy."

His face lights up and I'm already kicking myself. But when he falls into step right beside me, and the tight vise on my heart eases a little, I can't help but feel like this is okay. Not good, not great, but okay.

We've been married a long time. Together even longer. It's going to be complicated to untangle our lives, and we don't need to do it at DEFCON 1.

The first restaurant we poke our heads into isn't busy, so

Luke asks for a booth at the back. The server drops menus when she seats us, and promises to return with coffee momentarily.

It takes her nearly ten minutes, and they're the longest ten minutes of my life. Luke makes small talk, which he's not good at in the best of times. He asks about the show again, and I dodge the topic.

He brings up some book he started reading that morning about recovering from an affair, and I change the subject. I'm sure he just read the back of it and assumed he was the expert. That's how he rolls through life.

Why did you ever love this man? An excellent question, followed immediately by my insides rolling over as another thought flashes through my mind. It's going to take some time to fall out of love with him. I'll teach myself how, it'll be a fun project like launching my art career.

Because he can't read my mind, he's never been able to do that, Luke chooses that same moment to inch his hand closer to mine. I can feel the phantom warmth of his touch against my skin even with inches between us.

Traitor, I want to hiss at him.

Instead, my fingers flex, then flatten on the tabletop.

When I look up, his gaze is locked on my ring finger, which has been bare for a long time now.

He pulls his hand back, dipping it into his pocket, before pulling his own ring out. That's better than mine, I guess. I vaguely try to remember where my ring even is, which is an easier thought to grab on to rather than really thinking about why he brought his ring to see me.

The platinum band spins on the table between us.

"I know we haven't worn these in a few years..." His voice catches on the last two words. Has it been that long? I guess so. Time flies when you're miserable and numb.

I don't remember which of us took it off first. I do remember why, though.

"Why didn't we break up three years ago?" I ask abruptly.

Luke's face clouds over. "Because we love each other."

I laugh. It's the only reasonable response.

"Come on, Grace," he mutters under his breath as the server finally makes her way in our direction.

We're both silent as she pours coffee and takes our order.

As soon as she's gone, Luke leans across the table. It's not fair, he's big enough he can get close to me without trying. "I want to fight for us. Fight with me. Tell me what I need to do."

I shake my head. "I'm just here to eat some food before I go to work. You tagged along."

HE LETS IT GO, and we eat, but after, as we back to our cars, he's practically vibrating. I know he's going to try again, and I just want to get to work.

I'm tired. He looks tired, too. This is not a good idea.

Don't, I say in my head, which is how I have most conversations with him, apparently, because I'm exhausted just imagining saying half this shit out loud. Instead, I burrow deep inside myself and imagine what my life would be like if I hadn't sat next to him in the cafeteria and told him I thought his answer the day before had been really good, actually.

Grace Dunn, propping up Luke Preston's fragile ego from day one.

I unlock my car from a few feet away, and reach for the door handle.

Luke steps forward and puts his hand on the car, the same way he'd tried to block me leaving the bedroom yesterday. I glare up at him. "Don't do this again."

He ducks his head and mutters something.

"What?"

"I just want you to fight for us."

It's the way he repeats the same pathetic plea he made in the restaurant, like we hadn't agreed to let the conversation go. It makes my head explode. *Fight for us.* That's all I've done for the last twenty years. I have protected him, I have protected his family. I have loved him when he is the most imperfect man ever.

I have wanted him desperately. And he has never returned any of that effort, not nearly enough of that desire. And now he wants me to keep fighting. I have fought enough.

"Are you kidding me?" I burst out. "If you want us to survive this somehow—and frankly, I don't think that's possible—*you* have to fight for us. I'm done. You want *me* to fight for us with you? I've already done my part. Now it's your turn, *you* spend the next twenty years fighting for us. The way that I have fought for us. And then *maybe* we'll be even. Okay? Enough of that. Don't dump yet another problem in my lap.

Another Luke-fucked-up and Grace-will-fix-that situation. That's not what this is."

"That's what I mean," he cuts in, his breath surging out of him now as he bends at the knee, trying to keep eye contact with me. "I'm saying this all wrong. I don't know what the right thing to say is. But I want to fix it. Do you want me to fix it?"

"I don't know what I want." I'm numb inside. "I know that I wanted you desperately. I loved you far too much. Right now, I just want to get my show going. I just—you know, for a long time I have supported your career, through good and very bad."

The numb feeling is warming into some sizzling anger again. I'm so tired of this cycle.

I roll my neck, exhale, and shake it off. "Now it's my fucking turn. I need you to get out of my way for a little bit. That's what I want. I don't have the energy to fight about this right now. What I need is to work. And it's going to be really fucking challenging as it is, so please don't make it any harder."

"Okay. I hear you."

"And I need you to get out of the apartment, because I can't sleep at Sam's again." I gesture in the direction of his brother's building. "I'm not ready to explain…"

He swallows, his eyes wide, and he nods. "I'll go to a hotel."

"Look for something more long term than a hotel," I mutter.

He steps back, and I open the door to my car. Then I close

it again, swearing, because I need to put Sam's sheets in the fucking dryer.

"What is it?"

I shake my head, and he follows me to Sam's building.

"Go away," I tell him, exasperated.

"Maybe I'll stay here," he says as I use the key fob I should probably stop using. Sam and I have had a co-dependent relationship for too long, and he's in a relationship now. I'm no longer his stand-in mother or big sister, and he's no longer my safe space.

Ergo, his apartment is no longer my safe space.

My heart aches a bit as I realize that, albeit not for the first time. It's been an adjustment process for me because I'm so fucking needy. And as it turned out, I had good reason to be needy, because my husband was fucking around.

"Unless you don't want Sam to know we're struggling."

"Separating."

"Temporarily."

"Permanently." I sigh as the elevator takes its time to arrive. "You can tell him if you want to. He'd let you stay here. He'd love an excuse to go to Hazel's full time."

Luke doesn't say anything to that.

He doesn't speak again until we're in Sam's place, and I'm turning over the laundry. "I'd rather not tell him," he admits. He shrugs. "I don't want to tell anyone. But if you want me to, I will."

I roll my eyes.

Likely story. I keep telling him to leave me alone and he

ignores that. Why am I letting him follow me around like a puppy?

I come to a stop, staring at the button on the dryer. *Run cycle.* Why *am* I letting Luke do this? I turn around slowly and glare at his back. He's standing at the window in the living room, which has the most amazing view of the CN Tower.

"This is a great apartment," Luke says without turning around. "You did a good job picking it out for him."

"He chose it. I just helped."

"Why *haven't* you told him? I thought you would have called him."

"About the affair?" My mouth goes dry. "I don't know."

Because Sam doesn't want to know my drama anymore. Rejected by Prestons at every turn.

He finally twists on his heel and looks at me, his expression unreadable, but he shows his hand, anyway. "Because it would make this final."

"No."

"But yes, maybe."

"That's not it," I snap.

I've given myself away.

"No?"

"Shut up."

He doesn't bite.

I'm tired and sad, and I want Luke out of my space, but I'm not ready to tell the world, either. It's not just Sam. This is my own personal hell I'm trying to survive. I don't need gawkers, people who mean well, caregivers, friends, fans, or foes to have any clue of what I'm struggling with.

I don't want Caitlyn to know I'm struggling, either.

I gasp quietly.

I'm not admitting that to Luke for sure. I don't want him to know I even know her name, have looked her up. Better that he think it's all about his brother.

"All right, I don't want Sam to know because it will be final then. Yes."

"He'll take your side." Luke doesn't sound upset, but it's still hard to interpret his expression. He's made a career of being unreadable, even when desperate.

I nod. Yes, Luke's brother would choose me in a divorce, no question. It hurts my chest to think about. "I can't do that to you."

"You always wanted us to have a closer relationship than we ever did."

"You own a firm together. You are closer than you think. And you are all the other has."

"He has Hazel."

"He's all *you* have, then."

The corner of Luke's mouth pulls up, a sharp slice of misplaced optimism. "I have you."

"No." That boundary is so hard to maintain while I'm letting him follow me around to breakfast and this laundry errand.

As if he can read my mind, he dips his head and tries again. "As a friend, then."

I take a deep breath. "Yes. That's fair. I don't like you right now, to be clear—"

"That's clear as hell."

I will not laugh. I cannot laugh. I bite the inside of my cheek. "But I want the best for you." And because I'm not that altruistic, I layer in some snark. "Even if you don't want it for yourself."

A direct hit. Those shouldn't give me as much pleasure as they do.

Stop hurting him.

I will. Later.

"I guess I deserve that."

I frown. "Stop that."

He hunches his shoulders and now he won't look me in the eye. "You just said—"

"I'm aggrieved. I have the right. You need to be kinder to yourself." I take another deep breath— I'm so tired of breathing deeply, calm blue oceans—and move to the door. I'll let Sam think the sheets in the dryer are there because he did laundry. I need out of this apartment. I need to get away from Luke before I say something else kind and he takes it the wrong way.

He follows, standing too close as we wait for the elevator. As it opens, he leans in and murmurs, "I really do hear you, you know."

Time will tell. "Good."

"I'll let you know when I'm out of the apartment later?"

I don't turn my head to look at him. I stare straight ahead and nod. "Thanks."

In the lobby, I march straight ahead, trying to outpace him, but he has longer legs than I do. When I get to the sidewalk, he's right beside me again.

"Thank you," he mutters. "For not telling Sam."

"For now," I tell him. "I'll keep this secret for a while. For my own reasons, not for yours. But you need to take care of yourself, and get some help, because we are going to tell him at some point soon."

"What do you mean, get some help?"

I unlock my car for the second time this morning, and this time I'm first to the door. I pull it open. "Therapy, Luke. You're all messed up, and not my problem anymore. It's time for you to pay someone to care about your feelings."

1 0

LUKE

"Tell me why you're here."

I glance around the therapist's office on the second floor of a converted house just off College Street. Getting straight to the point. "My wife found out I was having an affair a week ago. It was the worst day of my life. I moved out, because she needs space, but she told me to get some therapy." I let out a rough breath. "So I'm here. And I want to do this for me, I guess, but also for us. I want to figure out where I went wrong, so I can maybe show her I won't do it again."

"You want to repair your relationship."

"Yes. And I don't know how."

"Is that something she's interested in?"

I hesitate. "I need to do this. I need to try."

"Why?"

"Because I love her." The words rip from my chest and leave a wound. "I know how that sounds. Why would I cheat on her if I love her?"

51

"It's a good question."

"Why does anyone do anything?"

"Like what?"

I shrug. "You tell me."

He nods. "Okay. Well, I mean, we could start with your childhood."

I tense up.

He notices. I notice that he notices, and he scribbles something on the notepad he's holding. "Maybe we'll come back to that. How about substance use?"

"I drink a bit."

"How much is a bit?"

"Not daily."

"And when you drink?"

"My brother is a gambling addict," I blurt out. "We know about addiction."

"Have you been treated for something like that?"

"I don't have that same addictive personality," I mutter.

He nods. "And sex?"

My mind goes blank. I swallow hard. "Excuse me?"

"Was the affair sexual?"

Flashes of mistakes. Regret. "Yes."

"Can you tell me about it?"

"The affair?"

"Yes."

No. My chest hurts. "It was a mistake."

"You mentioned that." He shifts positions. "We'll come back to that, too. You mentioned that you love your wife. What does love mean to you?"

"I think that's changed in the last week."

A pause. "Interesting."

"It's like I woke up from a bad dream. There's old Luke, and I'm looking at him, who he became. Like we branched from the same trunk person, who I used to be, but I don't recognize myself like that. That's not who I want to be. It's not who I am right now. I'm—I spent last night sobbing in the shower. I've never cried like that before. And it's fine. It felt gross, but it was necessary. The new Luke cries."

"And thinks crying is gross."

"New Luke is still working on word choice."

"I cry," he offers. "It's cathartic. It feels good."

"I'm not there."

"That's okay. It's a process. And so is repairing your relationship with your wife. But that's a two-party process. She needs to decide what she wants. You can't make her try to repair the relationship if she isn't interested."

"I know that."

"Do you?" A small smile tugs at his mouth, but it doesn't feel like he's laughing at me. His eyes are warm, creased with lines at the corners.

I think he understands. *Did you ever fuck around on the perfect woman? Did you ever blow your life up for no good fucking reason?*

"I do," I say haltingly. "I get it. But we have a bond. We have —had—a really good relationship. It just went off the rails a few years ago. And I need to be better to her. But she loves me. I know that deep down."

"That sounds confident."

"I don't lack in ego."

He makes a non-committal noise and scratches something on his notepad.

"Tell me about your wife."

I frown. We're not going to dig into the ego thing? But I'd rather talk about Grace any day. "She's amazing."

"What else? What would the old Luke have said?"

"Which one?" College Luke was in awe of Grace, too. When did we lose that?

"The one who had an affair. What would he say about Grace?"

"She's too good for me." I'm getting used to the poignant pause after I say something significant. I shift in my seat. "She's elegant. Smart. Successful."

"What made you bristle?"

"Stupid shit."

"Was it stupid to you then?"

"I had a short temper. I'd pick fights with her."

"And now?"

"I want to learn how to communicate better. I want to figure out why I picked fights with her."

"Do you think it might have anything to do with the fact she's elegant, smart, and successful?"

"No." I scowl. "She's also warm, funny, sexy."

"And you value those things more."

"I didn't say that."

He nods. "No."

Fuck. "I never meant…"

"Do you still see her as elegant?"

I picture her face, tear-stained and puffy, asleep on our bed. "Yes."

"Remote?"

I jerk my head up and glare at him. "I never said I thought she was remote."

"Aloof? Cold? I'm just asking. Those are sometimes synonyms for elegant."

"This isn't her fault."

"No. You made a decision you regret. This is all about you. But it's also about the stories you tell yourself to justify that decision. You need to unpack all of it, including the negative things you thought about your wife then. Turn them around."

I STOP at the bookstore on the way home and buy every book on the reading list the doc gave me. Then I pick up a grocery order, because I don't plan to leave my temporary lodgings for a few days. The less I come and go, the better.

It's a solid plan in theory. But it gets blown out of the water when I pull into my parking spot, and Grace is walking across the garage from the private access elevator at the same moment.

She frowns. "What are you doing here?"

I shrug.

"Luke..."

"I found a place a stay," I tell her. It's the truth.

"Then why are you here?" She's dressed for work. Faded jeans, long-sleeved t-shirt. A duffle bag slung across her small body. She looks like she did when I first met her, a gorgeous little art student, way out of my league.

Still true.

"I've rented a place."

Her eyes narrow. "Where?"

I shrug again.

"Luke!"

"There was an empty loft on the second floor." As I say it out loud, it sounds less clever than it felt when I discovered it on the leasing agent's website.

Grace purses her lips, takes a deep breath, then matches my shrug with a coolly indifferent one of her own. "That's a choice, I guess. That will get awkward when I start dating."

My mouth runs dry. "Are you…"

She rolls her eyes. "You have no fucking right to finish that question."

"Fair." I shove my hands in my pockets so she can't see me ball them into fists. "Yeah. I guess that'll be hard for me. I need to live with that."

She keeps glaring at me like that will make me back off. Like I'll be scared of a *look*. But the thing is, she's *looking* at me. I don't care why. If she's looking at me, she might see me.

Or maybe I'm hinging all my hopes on something she's done for two decades that never made a difference before.

You didn't let it make a difference.

Well, now I'm going to be a different man. Slowly. Over time. I move to the trunk of my car and open it. Giving her the space to walk past me to her car.

She gives me a wary look, expecting me to get in front of her again, stop her in her tracks. Force her to talk to me.

I want to, of course, but it won't work. The doc's words reverberate in my head. *"She needs to decide what she wants. You can't make her try to repair the relationship if she isn't interested."*

"I'm in 2B," I offer. "If you ever want to talk."

Then I grab my shopping and head for the lobby.

It feels like I handled that well. I get settled with my reading, and the afternoon passes.

When I hit a rough chapter about the relationship between fathers and sons, and tears prick the back of my eyelids, hot and uncomfortable, the therapist's words again ring in my head.

Cathartic. This doesn't feel cathartic. It's deeply uncomfortable.

Cathartic was letting Grace look at me with anger burning in her eyes. *That* at least feels like it's getting me somewhere. Like maybe she could singe me to a crisp so I could rise from the ashes.

Crying just makes my eyes hurt.

I jump off the couch, leaving the book behind. That's enough reading for one day. I need some food.

I'm halfway to the small kitchenette—these lofts were not created equal—when there's a knock at the door.

My heart fucking *leaps*, like God answered my fucking prayer, and I sprint to open it.

Grace is on the other side, still in her studio clothes.

She's looking down at her phone, rage radiating off her.

My heart sinks as I stand in the doorway, waiting for her to look up, realizing that she's not going to.

"You fucking asshole," she hisses, her hand shaking, her face still hidden. "Why does she call you Master?"

And just when I thought it couldn't get any worse, it does.

11

GRACE

I CAN'T BELIEVE it took me a week to actually read some of the text messages I'd taken screenshots of, *actually* read them, carefully, word by word.

Something about the way Luke behaved in the garage earlier made something in my brain go...wait a second. It took hours of sculpting for the thought to surface properly, that instinct to go look again at the text messages.

And there it was, in one message. She called him master.

There's only one reason for that, and I want fucking answers.

"Come inside," he says, trying to touch my arm.

I shrug him off and step into the spartan bachelor loft. He's clearly bought some furniture. A couch, a bed. No table or chair. No TV.

There's a book on the couch and his laptop and work papers are strewn across the bed. It looks like a nicely finished dorm room.

Oh, how I wish I'd made different choices twenty years ago.

The door clicks shut behind me. I pull a letter from my pocket and hand it over. I've already taken pictures of it.

"I went through your stuff last week. Somehow I missed this. Maybe it fell out when you were packing."

He opens it, then drops it, his face going ashen. Good. I hope he feels like the monster that he is.

I lift my chin. "I'll find everything. I'm smarter than you think."

"I think you're the smartest person in the world," he says dully. It doesn't sound like a compliment.

"You claimed you wanted to fix us," I say, my voice shaking. "While you were writing her shit like that?"

"It's not what you think," he says, his voice thick and hitching at the end.

I glare at him. "She called you Master."

"It's just a…sex word. A name. It doesn't mean anything."

How gullible does he think I am? "And you call her Kitten. With a capital K. Capital M. Capital K."

"So what?"

Hysterical laughter bubbles up from deep inside my aching chest. "You're her Dom, Luke."

He blanches. "What?"

"You're. Her. Kinky. Fucking. Dom."

"How do you…"

"Because I *know*, you asshole! Because I wasn't born yesterday, because I have the internet, because I read things, because…" God, my mouth is dry. I lick my lips and try again. "Because…"

Heat swarms through me. I can't do it. I can't explain to him how I know, when he should know that already.

I stumble forward, twisting around as I move through his new apartment that's far too close to our loft. The home I wanted to rebuild for him. The space *I* bought with the erotic art I made, inspired by *him*.

"Sit down," he says behind me, his voice distant.

His hands try to land on my shoulder and I turn away from him, dropping onto the couch.

I grab the nearest pillow and clutch it to me. "I want you out of this building."

"Let me fix this." His voice is low now, but his breath is harsh and shallow. He's trying to keep control of this, but he has no fucking idea what control is.

He doesn't understand me at all. What I want.

"Tell me everything," I say woodenly.

"I don't know what you want to know."

"Everything. I want to know every little perverted detail. You and your slut mistress have secrets, from me, and I want to know them all."

"It wasn't as kinky as you think. She liked those words."

I like them too, not that my husband would know that. I wipe away furious tears I refuse to let fall. "Do you remember when I first asked you to spank me? How shy I was about that?"

He groans, a feral sound that tries to break my heart. I won't let it. "It wasn't like that, baby. Nothing like that."

"Do you remember?"

"Of course I do."

"And you were so resistant. You didn't want to hurt me."

"I never want to hurt you."

"You hurt me when you fucked her. You hurt me when you stopped fucking me. You hurt me when you fucked me again, knowing you'd just fucked her, and so it was weird. You have hurt me every day over the last two years, you miserable sack of shit."

"I know. I'm sorry."

"There have never been two emptier words than *I'm sorry* spilling out of the mouth of a lying fucking cheat."

He doesn't repeat it, and that's good.

I glare at him, and he glares back, his eyes wet. "I don't want to lose you, Grace."

"Then why did you fuck someone else?" My voice cracks. "Why did you call someone else Kitten?"

His mouth drops open, and he shakes his head. "I don't know."

I lunge at him, shoving the pillow in his face. He catches my arms, absorbing the blow, and I break into a thousand sobbing pieces.

12

LUKE

Three years earlier

THE ACID CHURN in my gut is worst at night.

I've never slept well, but since Sam's sentencing and the plea bargain that kept my brother out of jail—and the gutting of our bank accounts that went hand in hand with that, the non-stop critical inspection of our books by regulators, and the fact he's sleeping on my fucking proverbial couch, *still*— my insomnia's gotten worse.

Grace is still at the studio when I get home from the office.

Sam is in the guest room.

Fine, it's not a fucking couch.

It's still too much.

Tomorrow, the regulators will be back to review my plan to bring him back to work in a limited, no-trading capacity.

The little shit needs a fucking job.

I chew a couple of Tums as I strip off my clothes and start

the shower.

GRACE COMES HOME AN HOUR LATER, with dinner for all three of us. Sam emerges from his room but barely says a word as we eat. Fine by me. I don't say anything, either.

Grace gets on my case when we retreat to the bedroom. "You could make an effort, you know."

"I don't need you telling me how to be a brother," I snap.

"That's not what I'm—" She cuts herself off and strips off her clothes, then pulls on a tank top and panties.

"If you're going to bark at me, the least you could do is make it sexy," she quips. "Threaten to spank me or something."

I frown and get into bed, ready for a futile attempt at sleep.

She gives me an uncertain look, but crawls closer anyway. "Come on." Her voice drops to a shy, hesitant note. It pricks at the back of my brain and feels dangerous. "Spank me, Luke. Channel some of that pent-up aggression in a more productive direction."

The only thing pent-up inside me is irritation, and there's no channeling that into being some kind of sex stud on command. "I'm not—I don't want to."

"Hey," she says softly, stopping. But her gaze is challenging. It's always challenging, because I'm never enough for her. "What if I want it?"

I make a face. "Don't be weird about it. I don't want to do that."

"Oh." She changes direction and crawls to her pillow instead, tucking her wee little self under the blanket. And then she rolls onto her side, facing the wall.

Giving me her back.

Well, I asked for that. I move closer, setting my hand on her shoulder. But she hears my sigh and takes it the wrong way.

"Don't make me feel like a freak," she whispers.

"I don't know why you always need to make it about sex."

"Because we're married, and married people have sex. You used to be a guy who liked sex. What happened?"

I didn't know my libido was so tightly tied to being a business success. "Nothing's happened."

"Great. Then it's just being a freak."

"That's not what I said."

"It's what I hear."

I sigh again. I'm so fucking tired.

"I have to leave early tomorrow," I mutter.

"Do you want me to set my alarm?"

"No."

"Okay." Two very small sounding syllables. One word that's a complete lie. None of this is okay, but I can't fix us until I get Sam back on track.

I lay beside her as her breath goes even. Then I curl up behind her, trying not to think about all the ways I've failed her and the mess that still needs to be untangled.

And in the morning I go into the office to meet two lawyers from a new law firm we're considering hiring as outside counsel.

13

GRACE

Present day, sobbing on Luke's couch

LUKE HOLDS me as I pummel his chest with my hands. He doesn't try to stop me, and when I collapse against him, exhausted, he kisses the top of my head.

It's infuriating.

But more than that, it's utterly depressing, because where was this man three years ago?

"I had my first therapy session this morning," he says when I'm finally quiet.

I move off him, and he catches my wrist, then lets go when I look down at the contact point.

He sighs. "That note you found. I never gave it to her."

"What?"

He gestures to where it lies on the floor. "I wrote it. I'm deeply ashamed of that. But it didn't feel right, and I never gave it to her. That's—you can see that, right? If it was in my things, it's because I never gave it to her."

"There were probably more."

"There weren't."

"I'll never know that, though. I'll always know that I love you more than you love me, that my love exists on a deeper, more painful level than yours. Because instead of diving deep into the pain, you scurried away."

"I'd never leave you. I love you. I never stopped loving you."

"Your definition of that word is different from mine. You want to know something truly awful? You don't know just how much you love someone until they rip your heart out. Until they take your fidelity and make a mockery of it. And when you stay with them, when you can't leave, not really, not even when you God damn fucking want to... *That's* pure, unconditional love. And it's the worst feeling in the world." I laugh. I'm on a fucking roll now. "Unconditional love isn't to be held in esteem. It's a trap. I love you without reservation, without conditions. I should have kicked you out that night, that very second that I found the text messages. Made you go far, far away. You can't be this close to be, because now, I find myself back here. Willing to take anything you dish out, apparently. I find a note, realize what a text message says, and I come scurrying downstairs to talk to you about it. We are a dysfunctional mess, Luke."

"I'll never do it again. I don't want to. I don't—" He takes a deep breath. "It was the worst collision of events. Things weren't good between us."

"I'm aware. We had a number of brutal fights about it. But you promised me that things would get better after Sam moved out, and it all just got worse instead."

"I don't know why."

"And I don't care why, now. Go fuck yourself. I wanted that kink, and you gave it to her."

"I didn't. Not really. It was playacting. We've had better sex than that, Grace. We've had…" He licks his lips. "There has been…"

But he can't say it.

It's not like we didn't have a good sex life.

Well, no. We didn't have a *good* sex life. But we had a very decent one. I wanted it to be better, because I'm a stupid fool.

But at no point when he was fucking her—Caitlyn, the name I'll never get out of my head—he never stopped fucking me.

It just got weird.

And bad, more often.

Sometimes good, though, and it's those moments I replay viscerally, as if there is some meaning in the way he occasionally wanted me *ever so*, in between all the times he found me not quite enough.

"I can't explain it. There is nothing that makes it right."

"You wanted her more than me."

"No. I wanted her less and told myself it was better that way."

"Why did you stay with me?"

"Because I love you."

I shake my head. That doesn't make any sense. "You don't

like what I like, if we aren't interested in the same big… Luke, when I talk to you about art, you look bored. And when I brought up kink, you look terrified."

"I'm not. Maybe I was, but that was for stupid reasons. I want to know more about what you like."

I can't believe that. "I can't trust you," I whisper. "Ever. You will never be the man I want."

"Tell me about him. Tell me what you want."

"I want a man whose mouth drops open when I strip down and I'm wearing lingerie. I used to strip in front of you and you didn't even fucking notice. I want a man who finds my kinky interests exciting, not terrifying. I want a man who doesn't run scared to another woman when things get tough, and stay there, fucking her, until he's found out. You, Luke, are not what I want."

He nods, his shoulders bunching, then sighs and changes the subject. "My therapist asked if you're seeing someone."

I shake my head. "Not yet. I will."

"Good."

"Not for you. Not for us. I'll go see someone for *me*."

"I'm here if you want to talk."

"I don't."

"But you came to find me."

"To confront you." I point at the letter, my finger shaking. "That. The text messages. Your secret kinky life."

"It wasn't that kinky."

"It was more kinky than you ever let yourself be with me."

"Because I was scared," he snaps.

I sit back, his anger the splash of ice water I needed. "Ooh, hello Luke. It's been a week since I've seen you. But there you are. Push comes to shove, and Luke shoves back."

"I'm a human being," he says gruffly. "I have emotions. I'm not mad at you."

"Then what are you mad at?"

"Myself!" He shoves a hand through his hair. "You don't think I want to do kinky shit with you? I don't even know what you want, and I want all of it."

"Because you've lost your mistress."

"I have forgotten she ever existed. You kicked me out, Grace. Remember? I don't live with you anymore. This is the extent of my life, and I still want you. Only you. I've fucked up, but I'm still here. Whenever you're ready, *if* you're ever ready, I want you. Just tell me how."

14

LUKE

I DON'T SEE Grace again for four days. I've started following her online, so I can see from her Instagram stories that the countdown is on to her art show. She's going back and forth from the studio to the gallery.

Then, out of the blue, she texts me.

Grace: I need a favour.
Luke: Anything.
Grace: You said you didn't want your name attached to the show. I want you to do the exact opposite of that.
Luke: Okay. Just tell me what or where to go.

She knocks on my door ten minutes later. She's wearing a dress today, with tall boots and a rare full face of makeup.

I hope my expression reflects my awe at her beauty, but it probably doesn't, because I've failed at showing her how much I love the way she looks at every turn.

Stepping aside, I gesture for her to enter my lonely bachelor pad. "Do you want to come in?"

"I'm on my way to the gallery," she says in a rush. "But we're having trouble getting someone from *The Star* to cover the show, I think because of the erotic nature of it, maybe." She presses her lips together like she's going to say more, then changes the subject. "So I want you to pull whatever strings you can to leverage our connection. 'Wife of a Bay Street firm holds first show at a Toronto gallery' might be a better angle for a story."

"You want me to call the paper? Who would I call?"

"A business reporter you know?"

"I don't, really. We have a media manager at work—"

"Then use them," she snaps, and there's that flash of anger again.

"Don't you have connections?" I ask, which is entirely the wrong thing.

She stalks to the couch and flings herself onto it, crossing her legs. "Did it ever occur to you that Caitlyn might look at you—the long hours, zero recognition of your wife in public, no social media connection—and think, hey, maybe that's one un-fucking-happy marriage?"

I blink, slowly, then shake my head. "No."

"That wasn't a part of why you didn't want to celebrate what I do?"

"I— I don't think it was conscious, Grace. I do want to celebrate—"

"So what's your excuse now? Why are you looking me in the face when I'm asking you for help, and telling me I should do it myself? Don't you think I've tried my connections? It's not the same, Luke. I'm a commercial artist with a following on the internet. That means nothing to the Toronto establishment."

I exhale roughly. "Jesus, Grace."

"What? Jesus, Grace, why do you have to be so rough on the poor, innocent man who only banged his lawyer for a while instead of taking care of things at home?"

Scrubbing my hand over my face, I fight back the protest that wants to roar out of me. I feel every muscle in my face tense up and then release. My mouth goes tight and I see red, but then it fades.

Another exhale, this one soft and long and sad.

And she watches me, her expression shifting to match.

We keep going through these fights, like rounds in a boxing match, and they're exhausting. I shrug. "I don't know what to say."

"Say, I'll talk the show up on Twitter. I'll tag the right people and use my Forest Hill name to get you some press. Say, I'll pose for a picture for you when *The Star* comes to cover opening night, because you're going to make a phone call or two and get *The Star* to come to opening night."

I open my mouth and close it.

She crosses her arms over her chest, like she's not playing around.

Her dress slides up her legs, and the overhead lights glint off the delicate curve of her calf. Shiny, silky... I drag my attention away from her legs. "Yeah, I'll make those calls. I'll figure it out."

"And you'll make an appearance at the opening?"

"I wouldn't miss it for anything." I grab a pen and make a note, then show it to her. "It's the only thing on my agenda next week."

"Good." She crosses her legs again.

I can't stop looking at them. She catches the line of my attention. Busted. "You don't usually wear nylons."

She smiles at me like she has a secret. "Nylons?" She smirks. "I'm not wearing nylons, Luke."

I want a man whose mouth drops open when I strip down and I'm wearing lingerie. My gaze drops from her beautiful, fierce face to the fitted pencil skirt.

She's wearing stockings. A garter belt.

Fucking lingerie under a fucking fuck-me pencil skirt.

My wife is dressed for sex, has been dressed for sex this entire time she's sat across from me and discussed using me for publicity.

The pen I'm holding snaps in half.

She stands up, the corners of her mouth lifting in a satisfied smile. So be it. If the only way I can please her right now is by letting her hurt me, so fucking be it. "Bye, Luke."

The way my name drips off her tongue. Yes. I nod. "I'll see you later, Grace."

It's not my right to claim this yet, and it may not be healthy, but she's mine. I didn't see that for too long, I didn't value that the way I should have, but she is God damned mine.

And she's dressed for sex.

I see that. I see *her.*

15

GRACE

MY FINGERS SHAKE as I pull out my phone in the elevator. The look on Luke's face as his attention zoomed in on my skirt—to what was under my skirt—felt like such a fucking victory.

That's right, husband. Remember that I'm a sexual fucking being. Not just that, but I'm sexier and dirtier and a hundred times more clever than the—

I cut myself off.

She doesn't get space in my head in this moment.

Neither does he. This moment, this victory, is all mine. I throw my head back in the empty space and laugh as rough, relieved adrenaline courses through my veins. Fuck yeah.

I could run a marathon right now. Win a boxing match.

I am woman, hear me roar.

When I drag in a breath and stretch my arms, my skirt slides up my thigh. I look down and catch the bottom hem, pull it up. I look at the exposed edge of stocking.

I look at my phone.

My heart beats a little faster. My fingers shake as I swipe into the camera app and point the lens at my leg. All I see is skin. It doesn't capture how I feel, this hot, crazy recklessness.

It doesn't capture how I felt as I dressed this morning, my wild sense of self.

I need to be in the shot. I tap on the button to flip the camera. My face flashes onto the screen, red and embarrassed. I stare at myself.

I'm an artist. I know how to do this. How to take broken bits and find something beautiful in them. Taking a deep breath, I raise my arm over my head, leaning back against the cool metal and the slice of mirror in the middle of the panel.

I spread my thighs. The elevator is almost in the garage now.

The timer starts counting down on the screen. Three, two…

My wrist shifts back and forth as I frame the shot. One leg. Bare skin, the top of a stocking. A rucked up skirt and then my jaw, jutting stubbornly into the shot. This is me, this picture says. This is me, and I like to wear stockings.

Victoria Secret models are posed just so, and now so am I.

When the camera clicks, I let the breath that I was holding out.

The photo is hot.

Hotter still once I crop it square and add a filter. I'm tempted to post it to Instagram. I'd get all the love there. *You go girl* and *Damn, honey!* But it would be followed by *Your husband is damn lucky*, and yes, he is, but he doesn't know it.

Doesn't appreciate it. And I don't need to hear that bullshit right now.

I just don't.

I love my fans, but the illusion I've built is slowly killing me from the inside.

Instead, I save the photo. It's just for me.

Or at least, that's what I tell myself.

Twenty minutes later, when I park in front of the gallery, after looking at the photo for the third time, and realizing I'm still girlishly in love with it, I send it to Luke.

Fuck him.

I'm fucking hot and he lost sight of that.

DAMIEN NOBLE, a metalworker and one of the other artists in the show, is already in the gallery space when I arrive.

He's a beautiful, dangerous looking man who likes to flirt with women in tall boots, and that might be why I'm dressed the way I am today. He's not actually my type, but I'm hoping he's in a complimentary mood.

I want another hit of that feel-good adrenaline.

Damien does not disappoint. He whistles as I approach where he's installing a massive birdcage at the back of the gallery.

There are three of us in this show. Damien works with metal exclusively. I like a bit of that, but I'm more into mixed media. Wax, stone, fabric, glass, plaster, wood. All of it, plus metal sometimes. And the third artist is a painter. Her canvases are already on the wall, ready for the show. Now Damien and I are filling the rest of the space with our installations.

"It's looking great in here," I say as I come to a stop in front of him.

He winks. "It sure is. You dressed up today, I like."

There. *Thank you.* But that's as far as my flirting can go. I smile. "I had to go and sweet talk my husband into helping with the promotion."

"Ah." He grins. "And?"

"He's going to make some calls." I gesture to the birdcage. "This is going to be the hottest piece in the show. You'll have people fighting for it."

"They don't need to fight," he drawls. "I have five more in progress at my shop."

"Smart." I sigh. "I should do that. I have fans who would love a duplicate. I worry about depreciating the value, though."

"Hasn't happened to me yet." He leans in. "Only five in the world is still a pretty exclusive club, you know what I mean?"

"Mmm." It's something to think about for sure. It would be easier for me to recreate some of my existing pieces rather than start a whole new collection right now.

My brain is not up for being a full-fledged creator. But creative mechanic? I could swing that.

"Maybe we should grab a coffee sometime. Talk more about the business end of things. Compare...processes. Do you like visitors to your studio?"

I absolutely hate that. "It depends," I say with a coy smile. "What's in it for me?"

His eyes flash with a feral heat. "That's up to you."

The door swings open and Alex walks in. I twist away from Damien, not that I'm doing anything wrong.

If Alex notices my cheeks are pink, he doesn't say anything. He joins us and slings his arm over my shoulder. "How's my favourite artist doing?"

I laugh as Damien insists he's great, and Alex gives him the finger.

"But, Grace, I'm serious…" Damien grabs my hand and rubs his thumb over my wrist. There's no way Alex will miss that. "I want to talk business later."

"Uh huh," I murmur as Alex steers me away.

He brushes his lips against my ear. "I should have warned you about Noble. He's a bit…hedonistic."

"It's kind of the theme of the whole show," I murmur. "It's fine."

"He's harmless."

I doubt that, actually, but I'm not going to tell Alex I'm suddenly painfully aware of people who don't care about boundaries like marriage vows.

Obviously to my inner storm, Alex changes the subject. "Are you ready for the show?"

"Yep." This is safer territory, even though I'm not going to give him a completely honest answer. I give him a bright smile. "Can't wait."

He hesitates. "How's Luke?"

"He would be able to tell you best," I hedge.

"He's not taking my calls."

"Oh." I frown. "Well…"

"I don't want to pry," he says hastily. "If it's…personal?"

I lean into him and give him a hug. "You're a good friend, Alex. Give him some space, maybe."

"Is he going to come to the show?"

"We talked about that just this morning," I say, which is a factual statement that leaves out an entire novel worth of asterisks and caveats. "I think so."

He better. If Luke doesn't show up on opening night, I'm never speaking to him again.

BY THE TIME I get home, the plump, squishy part at the top of my thighs is bulging out the top of my stockings, and I'm glad nobody is around to see me strip out of the ridiculous outfit.

Climbing into familiar around-the-house clothes feels better.

I had fun with my little performance, but that's not who I am. I look at the text message Luke sent back to me immediately after I sent that photo from the elevator.

Luke: That's my beautiful girl. My one and only.

I wanted a reaction, and that's as good as I could hope for, but I hate it too.

What I actually want is Luke to want me like this, in bamboo lounge pants and a Sarah McLachlan tank top. I want him to want me because I'm fired up to to go back into the studio tomorrow and work up a production schedule for making copies of my most iconic pieces.

And I want to curl up on the couch with him and talk about the pros and cons of that plan.

There has always been a part of me that wants Luke to be more like Alex and Sam. That wanted, over the last four years, for *Luke* to be who I go to for moral support. I don't want that from his brother or his friend.

I wanted it from my husband.

And there is a wound, deep inside me, a festering, layered wound that won't be easy to heal around the fact that he was never that kind of a support to me. I desperately wanted it from him. Not from anyone else.

What does it say about me that even now, as I am so sure there is no path of repair in front of us, I still wish he was my go-to guy to talk about things.

Because it's a lie that he was *never* that person.

It's just been a very long time.

16

LUKE

Eighteen years ago

"WHAT DO YOU THINK?"

I wasn't listening, and Grace knows it. I stretch my arms wide and take a deep breath. "I drifted there."

She pokes me with the cap of her pink highlighter.

We're supposed to be studying, but my brain is in a fog. Before she can get us back on track, my phone rings.

I frown as I recognize the number, and Grace catches my mood shift. "Who's that?"

"My brother. Sam." I hunch my shoulders. "He's four years younger than me. Just started at boarding school."

"I still can't believe that's a real thing that people do."

"Rich people who don't like being parents have options," I joke, but it's true.

Another email comes in from Sam, telling me not to open the first one. Aw, man. I click in to the first message anyway, and it's a wall of panic and uncertainty. I swear under my breath and climb off the bed. "I have to go call him."

"Do you want me to go?"

I lean over and kiss her on the mouth, soft and slow. "Nope. I want you here all night. But he's a fourteen-year-old boy, and if he knows my valedictorian girlfriend is listening, he's not going to open up about his troubles."

"Why would he know that I was valedictorian..." She trails off and beams at me. "Were you bragging about my high school academic record to your little brother?"

"It's impressive."

"It's embarrassing."

"You don't look embarrassed." I lower my voice and slide my hand under her shirt, finding her bare breast and squeezing. "You look pleased."

"Mmm." She shoves me away. "Go. Be a good big brother, and then come back because I want to talk to you about something kind of weird."

WHEN I RETURN, she's on the phone, too, but she gets off. "I gotta go, Luke is back."

Then she crawls into my lap, grabbing my hands and shoving them up her shirt. My little hedonist. "Where were we?"

"You wanted to tell me something weird."

She licks her lips, and I lean in to capture the wet streak with my mouth.

"Luke," she whispers as we topple sideways.

"Yeah."

"Wait, I was serious."

"But then you did something sexy, and I couldn't help myself." I stretch out on my back and she climbs on top of me.

Biting her lip, she glances down at me and flutters her eyelashes.

I laugh. "What is it?"

"I want to draw a picture of you."

I give her my best raunchy grin. "Sure."

"Naked."

"What?"

"It's for a project..." She scrambles off me and lies down, putting her earnest face right up against mine.

Of course I'm going to say yes. I'll never say no to her.

Coming to university and falling in love on day three was not my plan, but Grace Dunn is the best thing that has ever happened to me, and I'll do anything for her.

"The English Lit department..." She blinks in my face. "Luke. You did it again."

"Sorry." I swallow hard. "I was just thinking that I really love you."

Shock rolls over her face. "What?"

I sit up. "It's okay if it's too soon. I just thought you might want to know. The last three months have been...you've saved my ass. And I can't wait to see you at the end of every day. I never want to let you go. Because I love you."

She kisses me hard on the mouth, whispering something

back that sounds a lot like *I love you, too*, but I'm not sure, because my heart is pounding so hard I can feel it in my ears.

After what Sam just told me, pledging my heart to Grace is a dumb move. But it's the truth, and if my parents want me to transfer to the London School of Economics, they're going to be disappointed. I'm not fucking smart enough to go there, anyway.

If it wasn't for Grace, I'd already be failing out of U of T.

So I yank my fucked up scatterbrain back and give Grace my full attention. "Start over again. What's this project?"

She smiles sweetly. "The English Lit department hosts it every year. It's called the Art/Lit Project, and writers and artists are paired together to create mutually reflective pieces. I want to participate as an artist, and the poet I paired with has written a piece about..." She trails her fingers down my belly, to the muscle that curves over my hip. Her fingertips walk a path along that ridge until she dips them under the waistband. Then she smooths her hand flat and rubs my flat, tense abs. "This."

"There's a poem about abs?"

She nods vigorously. "And I really love it, so I want to draw something amazing to go with it. So I need an amazing model. What do you think?"

I think I'm taking my clothes off and sitting still for a while.

17

GRACE

Present day, sitting on the floor of her closet

I STILL HAVE that sketch of Luke. It's not that great, but I framed it when we moved into our Forest Hill house, when I worked with an interior decorator to create the perfect entertaining home. She told me my art was best kept to the bedroom suite area, because it was so…extra.

Now, that extra work is all over my loft, because fuck being small.

I'm extra as hell.

But that first sketch is in a mirrored frame, designed to catch the light off the chandelier in my dressing room—one of the indulgent *Real Housewives of Toronto* type of things I kept when we moved. So it's still hung over my jewelry case.

I miss that Luke. He was my favourite. Those first couple of years were…magical. I swipe away tears and take a big drink of a glass of wine that has found its way into my hand as I've stomped down memory lane.

I wonder if Luke ever misses those early days. That simple apartment we moved into when his parents threatened to disown him, the way we took Sam in over holidays, when he didn't want to go home because his dad hated him.

The senior Lucas Preston hates both of his sons, because neither of them are biologically his. My understanding is that he and his wife came to a sort of understanding, and then she blew it out of the water when Sam came out looking not at all like either of his parents, and very clearly like a close family friend.

Fuck. Maybe I should have seen the infidelity train barrelling towards us years ago. When Luke went to work for the family firm, that mended their relationship…and small changes started to happen in *my* relationship that I didn't pay enough attention to at the time.

I push to my feet and go in search of the bottle of wine I opened for a top up.

I fill it unfashionably high. It doesn't matter, I'm drinking it fast tonight.

But the glass doesn't chase away the weird thoughts that won't get out of my head. The haunting, what-if thoughts. So I open my computer and open an incognito browser so I can search for *her* without leaving a trace, not that I think I'm leaving any kind of trail.

Not that it matters.

I'm just looking at publicly available information. Who posts what, who likes what…

I lose track of time, poking through her social media friends. Nobody I recognize. Nobody connected to Luke, either.

Time to pour another glass, because I've hit an obsessive wronged-wife treasure trove. All the men who like *her* posts. I click on all of their profiles and try to figure out if they're married.

Most are not.

Three are, and I scowl at the screen as I sip my second over-filled glass.

I pace away from the computer and order delivery. A banh mi sandwich from the place down the street. Ten minutes, they say.

I love the city.

Back to the computer, and one of those three married men has his page wide open to the internet.

And there are messages that she's sent him that are clearly talking about private dinners in the last week. Well, she moves fast. Or maybe she has multiple lovers at once.

Maybe you're drunk and drawing conclusions.

Maybe I don't care.

This asshole is just like Luke. Maybe worse, because he's doing it in public. My mouse hovers over his name.

Don't do it, says the wiser part of my brain.

Fuck it, says my heart. *Tell him off. What does it matter?*

It doesn't. The fear of God is good for him, maybe.

And before I can think better of it, I hit send on a snarky, judgement-laden message.

I WAKE up the next morning with a raging headache, for obvious reasons. Too much wine, too much screen time, not enough sleep or common sense.

With a groan, I grab a laptop and carry it to the kitchen. As I brew an extra-large cup of coffee, I open the computer and wince at the evidence on the screen of my wine-fuelled critique of a stranger's choices.

Then, because I'm a glutton for punishment, I refresh the page—and find myself blocked.

Well, that's probably for the best.

Luke would be horrified if he knew what I did. It's the worst kind of behaviour he abhors on the internet. I would feel bad about it if his own behaviour in private hotel rooms wasn't a thousand times worse, and maybe the asshole from last night will think twice about making the same mistake my husband has.

My thoughts swirl from Luke to Damien Noble, and the conversation the day before. Then back to Luke, Luke of old, Luke from college, who would be the first person I'd talk to about taking my business in a new direction.

I'm so tempted to call him. No, text him. That would be safer.

Just to run the question past him.

Would it be fair? To ask him for that attention, knowing I'm using him? But also, why do I feel like I need to be fair? He hasn't been fair to me.

What if I'm selfish and I just take what I want? I'm nervous about this show. How best to leverage it and still deliver orders to my online customers who fund my life. The show is about prestige, local recognition. It's about my *reputation*.

I want to go for a walk around my city, with my husband, and be selfish for a short period of time.

Maybe I have to be honest with him about that. I think about texting him or emailing him or calling him, and explaining what I want.

But something holds me back, and I don't. And then when I go out, there he is. On the elevator when the doors open.

"Hi," I say cautiously as I join him in the elevator car. "Were you coming up to see me?"

What were the odds?

His cheeks stain red. "I was heading out to get some fresh air, and I saw the elevator was being called to the eighth floor. I hopped on just in case it was you. I just thought I might see you for a minute," he finishes, naked longing in his voice.

I have wanted him to long for me for ages.

And now he does. And it doesn't feel good. It feels hollow and empty and sad.

I'm not sure how to reply to that. *I was thinking of calling you* feels cruel now, like I would be leading him on. *I wanted to talk to somebody. And that somebody is you. Why is that somebody you? Why is it always you?*

I opt for a smile instead.

"How's the prep for the show going?"

I don't have to bring it up. He's asking all on his own.

So I answer him honestly. As we arrive on the ground floor, I admit, "I'm nervous about it."

He steps off first, waits for me.

"Are you heading to the office?"

He shakes his head. "I'm still working from home." He stumbles over that last word and corrects himself. "Here, the apartment. I was going to get a coffee."

"Oh, I was—" I cut myself off.

He looks surprised. "Are you also going to get a coffee?"

I nod. "And then I was gonna go for a walk, and think about why I'm nervous and what I need to do next and how to get ready for this, how to maximize the opportunity."

I'm blathering, but I want him to ask the next question, too. I don't want to have to invite him to join me.

Will he? I don't know. This is what we are now, two strangers who were once lovers, who were once married, who are still married. Strangers married to each other. Unsure of what to say next.

He searches my face. "Do you want to talk about any of that? It sounds like a lot to consider."

"Yes," I say. Feels good to be honest, that simple, single syllable, yes. I want to talk about it.

And then I couldn't hold it in anymore. I went off. "Actually what I want is to get coffee and go for a walk. I think better when I walk. Does that make sense?"

He shoves his hands in his pockets, his shoulders hunching. He's so big, next to me. I used to love his size, and then I started to resent it. And now it's just a curiosity to me. What does it feel like to be him, so big next to me, taking up so much space and not knowing what to say.

"Is that too weird for you?" I ask.

He shakes his head. "No. Not weird." He smiles. "It's nice, but I don't want to overstep. If you're open for company, I'd love to be a sounding board."

LUKE

WE GET our coffee and then head down to the waterfront. It's cold today, but bright, and she's bundled.

I'm less prepared than she is for the wind coming off the lake, but that's what the hot beverage is for, and I shove my other hand in my pocket.

Grace gets right to the point. "One of the other artists in the show suggested something that has taken up residence in my head, like maybe it's a genius idea, or maybe it'll dilute my brand." She does a backtrack first, and explains some things I maybe knew, but didn't really pay close attention to. How she sets up her art auctions online, which pieces she sells at set prices, and how she manages more people wanting those commissions than she can ever keep up with.

"I mean, I make a really nice revenue stream from prints and merchandise, too. That gives everyone a chance to own a version of a piece, while still maintaining the rarity of the original item." She takes a deep breath. "But the possibility of earning three or five times the commission on a major item, simply by creating a few of them…"

"It's tempting."

"Very."

"Is that the only way you see to scale your business?"

"Outside of brand partnerships? Yeah, probably. As long as I'm the sole producer of the art, there will be limits. So I can focus on the reproducible parts, like merchandise, or I can work harder. Or faster, or both."

She makes a face, and I chuckle. "No, you don't want to do that."

"Right? But I also don't want to copy Damien just because he mentioned it. I'm just antsy. I want to make the most of this. I've tried to get a show for three years and galleries just wanted nothing to do with me. When Alex introduced me to his partner, it was a dream. Damien doesn't seem to have the same nerves here, so I think, whatever he's doing, maybe I should do."

"There are probably other artists out there who look at you and say the same thing, though." I take a sip of coffee. "Something we tell companies before they're ready to go public, but they're in that pipeline is, there are other companies who aren't even there yet. We can forget to look behind us when we're so focused on what's the next big step ahead."

She makes a face. "I don't like to look back."

Not when we have nothing but train wrecks in our recent past, no, I bet she doesn't. "Sorry, that was thoughtless."

"It's fine. It's a generally good point."

"That's what I'm here for. Being in the vaguely right vicinity of a topic."

"Do you remember that sketch of you I drew in university?"

"It hangs in your closet, of course I do."

"But do you remember..." She trails off. "I don't know. There was a vibe about that whole project. It was just a club thing, but it consumed me and gave me something to be passionate about. Everything that I have done in my career, and that's the moment I remember. It was a turning point. Even though it took me thirteen years to really get serious about art, that was the origin moment. After that project, I started taking more art classes, and..."

"You found the thing that would drive you. You just didn't know it would be a career. But it's always been your passion."

She stops abruptly and turns to look at the lake, moving off the path.

I'm horrified to realize she's crying.

She shakes her head when I try to say something. Whatever I was about to say—it's okay, don't cry, I understand—would have been all wrong.

"I'm still young," she finally mutters. "But I feel like I've started my life over again a few times now, and I don't want to. Not again. I really liked this one, Luke. The loft, the studio, the lake, being downtown." She turns and glares in the direction of our building, now in the distance.

"I wanted that life," she yells, startling the joggers around us, and an older couple walking down by the water.

I force myself not to be embarrassed. It doesn't matter. It's fine. I don't know why she needed to be quite so loud about it, but I understand the sentiment.

A sinking feeling drags the next question out of me. "Grace, how much of that life is tied up in your art?"

She turns around and starts marching down the path again. Fierce and frightened. Like a kitten, I think, and regret twists my insides into barbed wire.

We walk in silence for a while, then she slows. "We should go back."

"If you want."

"This hasn't been the business talk walk I advertised it to be."

"That's fine." I clear my throat. "Sam realized I'm not working at the office anymore."

"What did you tell him?"

"I'm going through some things. General mental health stuff. Probably a coward's way out of the conversation, but I wasn't…" It was too soon.

"It's okay. He hasn't said anything to me." She makes a face. "I guess I'll tell you if he does. It's probably better to wait until after the show, anyway. The last thing we want is a scene."

"Right." Although that's not really a Grace thing to say. That's a Preston concern, and she's only ever worried about those on my behalf.

"We should go back."

"I'm not in a hurry."

She rolls her head. "I'm just—this isn't what I thought—"

"What do you want from me, Grace?" I hope to tell my

voice sounds pleading. I'll do anything she wants, I just need to know what that is. "Let me in. At least as a friend."

"No."

"I'll be gentle."

She laughs bitterly. "I don't want gentle. I want safe."

Fuck me, I don't even know what my wife wants. "What do you mean, you don't want gentle? Is this about kink?"

She gives me a strange look, then shrugs. "Sure. Okay. I don't know how to answer that. I think it's just about life. And maybe my life, maybe *I* am kinky, in a bone-deep way you will never understand, because when it's this intrinsic to someone, you get scared. But it's okay if it's play acting. I don't know, Luke. But you scare me. Not in a threatening way, but in a dangerous way. I don't want a gentle conversation from you. I don't want friendship from you. I wanted a desperate, needy, possessive fuck from you, and that was never on the table. Not for me. But it was for someone else. I've had enough of gentle from you for a lifetime and it was all deeply dangerous to my psyche in the end. Do you want to know something highly embarrassing?"

How am I supposed to answer that?

She glares at me with challenge in her eyes. "No?"

"Yes," I shout back. Now I'm the one attracting attention. "I want to know everything about you, Grace."

"Well, that's new."

Shame roars inside me, loud and wounded. It's my old standard, the driving force that built a firm to rival my father's in just a few years—and then let my brother destroy it. But then I fucking rebuilt it.

I can rebuild my marriage, too. "Yeah. It is new. And desperate, and needy, and possessive. So if you want to see that inside *me*, let me assure you it's there. Maybe I'm the one who should start sharing embarrassing shit with you, right? How about that?" I stalk over to a garbage can and get rid of my coffee. Then I spread my arms wide. "I'm a stupid fucking man, Grace, but I love you. If you don't want gentle, I'll give you something else. Just give me a chance."

"You don't get it, do you? We were done a long time ago. That's why you had an affair. I even made a sculpture about it. I guess you'll see it on Friday night. There, that's something I haven't told you yet. Surprise."

My chest heaves. "What?"

"There's a..." She gasps. "It's kind of pathetic, really. I mean, the whole show is a love letter to a man who never deserved any of it, but it's a tragic kind of love letter, and the final piece is called *Death of a Marriage*."

"When did you..."

"Months ago. I told myself it was just art, inspired by the world around me, and I was telling a story. But I wasn't. Okay? Every piece I have ever made has been about us in some way, and that part of me knew we were over before...this."

"Or..." My chest hurts, but I fucking plow on. I have to. "Maybe that wasn't the end of us. Maybe that was the death of *a marriage* but not *us*. That was the crisis point, and now we're on the other side of that, and we're going to be okay. That's possible, too."

"We aren't going to be okay."

"We are going to be better than okay. We are going to be amazing. With a fractured past but a dazzling future."

"That sounds like something you read in a book."

"It is." I look right at her, and hold her gaze. "I've been doing my research about repairing from an affair."

"That also sounds like someone else's words."

"Then here are mine. My wife is an incredible artist. The toast of the town. You said that you think I'm bored around you? I felt dull and boring next to you. Not *bored*. Boring. I don't know what to say about your art, because it's beyond me. But knowing that it's based on us? I can't wait to see it, Grace. I want to see *Death of a Marriage*. I'm not scared of that. I'm scared of losing you, but I'm not scared to look at my mistakes."

"Why?" She laughs, but it's the edge of hysteria, the edge of tears, and I feel the same. "Why now? Why not sooner?"

"I don't know." My cheeks are wet.

She turns around again and looks back at downtown. "We should go back."

And that's how the conversation ends. We walk all the back in silence.

When we get back to the building, I ride to the eighth floor with her, and she doesn't tell me not to.

Baby steps.

At her door—our door, our loft, our home, that I lost—I reach for her. She freezes. At first I don't think she's going to let me touch her.

"You need a hug," I say quietly.

"Not from you."

"Maybe not. But I'm here. I'm offering."

"I don't need a hug," she says stiffly.

"Look, you said you don't want gentle from me, not anymore, and…I hear that. But you're a hugger, Grace. I get that I didn't give you enough in the past. I promise I hear that. I'd really like to make up for that at some point. But right now, I see my best friend tightly wound, and I'm thinking she hasn't had a hug in weeks."

"Alex hugged me yesterday."

"I stand corrected."

But her gaze lingers on my face. Wary, uncertain. Wanting.

"Was it a bone crusher, though?"

She bursts into tears. "Luke…"

I step closer. Not touching, but close. And I reach for her hand again. This time she doesn't tense up. I brush my knuckles against hers, then slide my hand up the sleeve of her coat. The contact, even through layers of fabric, instantly warms me inside.

For a second, I hover my hand over her hip, the shape of her familiar and wonderful and entirely off-limits. Then I wrap my arm around her and pull her in against my chest. As I press my face to the top of her head, I feel tears slip out again, and the fucking therapist was right.

It's cathartic this time.

She shakes inside my arms, and I squeeze her tighter. "Tell me when to let go."

She sobs and burrows her face deeper into my chest. I

curse myself, and that shame monster inside me growls and hisses, happy with the mess he's made.

But I'm going to fix it. Piece by piece.

When she finally nods and rocks back on her heels, I let her go.

"Thank you," she whispers, not lifting her head to look at me.

That's okay. It's going to be, anyway.

I squeeze her shoulder one last time, then step back towards the elevator. "I'll see you tomorrow."

Her head jerks up. "What's tomorrow?"

I give her a little smile. "Whatever you want. Maybe another walk. We can get more shit off our chest."

She laughs and nods. "Okay. Tomorrow."

THE MORNING OF THE SHOW, I do something I've been putting off for two weeks. I go to public health and get tested for sexually transmitted infections. It's an anonymous clinic, straightforward, and I'm told I'll have results within a week.

It's the first time I say out loud to another human being that my husband cheated on me. The nurse asks if I need any other resources, and I take a pamphlet on counselling.

"Has he been tested?"

"I don't think so."

"He should."

That really doesn't feel like my responsibility, but she's right. I stubbornly want him to come to that conclusion on his own. He keeps saying he wants to make things right, fix us, but that has to start with fixing himself and taking responsibility for the mess of his own life.

He stepped up with press support for the show, though. Better than I expected. On our walk yesterday he told me he'd arranged for *The Star* to do a spread on the show, as I asked, but his media manager at work had also made some calls to magazines, and he'd followed up personally with invitations to opening night.

It was more than I asked for, and almost too good to be true.

So I stupidly get my hopes up.

And yes, photographers show up mid-afternoon at the gallery to take daytime photos of the pieces. I get pre-show calls from reporters, and it sounds from their questions like the bent of the articles is in the direction I want: serious art with erotic undertones, an unexpected new star on the Toronto scene after commercial success, blah blah blah.

It's great.

But then the show starts, and Luke is nowhere to be seen.

I'm an idiot for hinging my happiness on him, of course. *I know that.* And yet a few days of regular contact and thoughtful conversation tumble me back into that idealistic place of wishing my husband wasn't a fragile man child.

His brother shows up, though. I'm standing with Alex when Sam and Hazel arrive. She waves energetically, bless her heart, and warmth floods my chest. I can do this. I have friends.

None of them know I'm dying inside, but it's a slow death. Subtle.

Someone else approaches and Alex introduces them. I lose sight of my brother-in-law and his girlfriend as Sam shows Hazel some of the Damien Noble work he got a sneak peek at when I first brought him to the gallery.

That was the last time I saw him, I realize with a start. Other than Alex and Damien, I haven't seen anyone since I found out about the affair.

And Luke.

And a nurse at public health, who advised me not to have sex with anyone until I got the test results back.

But I've avoided Sam, and even though I'm glad they're here, I'm also glad I'm too busy shaking hands to really talk to them.

The next person I see is Zeke Devereaux, owner of The Wheelhouse, and the patron of this show. He looks like a biker, but he knows more about the art world than I ever would have guessed from my past encounters with the kink club owner. I'm grateful for his patronage, and I make sure to tell him that when he brings two guests over to introduce them to me.

"Are you kidding me? I do this kind of thing selfishly. This helps me find the kind of members who can afford to fund the outreach programs Caro loves to put on."

Zeke's wife runs daytime programming for people who want to learn more about how to explore alternate lifestyles safely, and she's one of my most favourite people in the world. "You know I think that's amazing."

"Then we have a mutually beneficial arrangement." He shakes my hand. "And I just bought *Death of a Marriage*, by the way. It'll be going on display at the club."

That's my most expensive piece. I priced it high enough that I thought maybe nobody would want it, and I'd get to take it home.

That was before. When I thought I was in control of my marriage, and when or if I wanted it to end.

Now? I'm stunned. "Thank you," I say again. "Although it hardly feels like it's sufficient."

"Stop." He laughs, and I apologize again, and one of his guests—an American—comments that it's a very Canadian back and forth.

Zeke drifts away and I get into a deep conversation with the American about organizing shows from a distance, and it's only when she gives me her card that I realize she's a gallery owner in California.

"I'd love to talk about you bringing this show to San Diego," she says warmly.

I'm bowled over. "I'd love to," I admit. "But these pieces are all being sold."

"Some buyers don't mind loaning their pieces back to a collection for a show, if it increases the value of the piece. Something to think about."

Indeed. There's so much to this end of the art world that I still need to figure out. "Thank you, I'll be in touch."

Conversations like that slowly spin me from one end of the gallery to the other, and I'm out of breath when Sam and Hazel finally find me near the bar.

"Congratulations," my brother-in-law says, giving me a tight squeeze. "You made Hazel's night, too."

His cheeks pink as she bursts into an excited story about meeting Zeke Devereaux for real this time.

"He's a pretty cool guy," I say. Then I lean in. "We should

get coffee so we can talk more freely about the kink world without Sam combusting right next to me."

"It's fine," he grumbles.

Hazel claps her hand. "I'd love to catch up."

We're picking a date when all the oxygen in the gallery seems to suck towards the door.

My heart lodges in my throat as I turn and see Luke standing in the entrance. He catches my gaze and nods, then takes in the fact that I'm standing with Sam and Hazel.

We're Prestons. We can't make a scene.

So when he joins us, he gives me a quick kiss that sears the corner of my mouth and steals my breath. *He's supposed to kiss me. He's my husband.*

Then he plants a hand in the small of my back and rubs a reassuring circle there as I stare up at him, scared to look anywhere else, unable to look at Sam lest he figure out that we're fighting again, but this time it's different, this time Luke has gone too far, this time I can't handle him kissing me.

Why did he kiss the corner of my mouth? Why not my head? I love the way his lips feel brushing my temple.

God, pull it together, Grace.

Luke is shaking Sam's hand, which is a weird thing they do, but again, Prestons. Are. Weird.

Hazel is watching me, then she leans into Sam and smiles. "We should get going."

Like she knows something is wrong, and she's protecting Sam from it. I can't say I blame her. I nod, and remind her that I do want to have coffee soon.

When we're alone, Luke steps back a little, giving me a bit

more space. "I'm sorry I'm late," he mutters under his breath. "I was working on something and time got away from me."

Old Grace would let him off the hook. That's not me anymore. "I was worried you weren't going to make it."

"I felt like shit when I realized how late it had gotten. And then I had to shave and shower and…" He glances around. "I haven't missed the press, have I? They said they'd be here toward the end of the night. I wanted it to be really busy when—"

"They haven't come back yet. That part is fine."

He exhales sharply. "Good."

"Do you want a drink?"

"No, I'm good." He glances around. "I want to see the show. Do you have time to take me through it? Is there a booklet? How does this work?"

"We'll be interrupted as we go, but as long as that's okay…"

He wraps his hand around my elbow, turning me so we're looking right at each other. "This is all about you. I just want to watch and celebrate."

My arms are bare tonight, I'm wearing a silky, sleeveless black turtleneck over my favourite skinny black trousers, and I thought it was a perfect artsy outfit, the right mix of conservative and unexpected. I hadn't thought about what it would feel like to have my husband pressed against me, his hands on my bare skin.

I can't breathe.

I want to arch into him, have him tighten that grip to the point it leaves marks.

That's not what we have. That's not what I am to him.

Another thought, one even more dangerous, whispers so quietly I can't really hear it. I twist away from Luke, grabbing his hand because that's better than him holding my arm, and I drag him to the front of the gallery.

Booklet. Check. "Here you go."

I shove it into his hands, and he nods. "Right. Alex gave me one of these. Sorry, I forgot." He gives me a sad smile.

Nope, we're not doing sad right now. I squeeze his fingers. "It's all good. So this is my first piece…" I slide into my shtick, the narrative that is mostly true and safe for public consumption. It falls apart when we get to the back of the gallery, but it takes us almost an hour to get there, and by then, I'm used to having him stand next to me and look at my creations, my heart's deepest desires come to life in three dimensions outside my body.

And then it's time for the final piece.

I've caught him looking at it already.

Death of a Marriage.

It's poured plaster, with metal and fabric embedded in it. It's the same pose Luke struck for me eighteen years ago. His body is bigger now, and in the sculpture, it's even bigger than he is now. This is Luke at the worst of the firm's crisis, when he was thick around the middle, not taking care of himself. Some of that weight had fallen off in the last year, and even more dropped since I found out about the affair.

The arms wrapped around him are mine. I cast them from a rubber mold that I made by actually embracing the plaster body.

I love it, and I hate it. I had felt such liberation when I made it six months ago, but then I didn't leave him.

I'm not as brave as this creation. *Fly, my lovely. Fly far away.*

But I don't.

Luke stands in front of it silently for ages. Then he clears his throat gruffly. "That's…"

"It was…" I can't.

He wraps his arm around me, his fingers caressing my shoulder. "It's brave."

"I don't know about that." I twist away again. "I'm going to get a drink."

He follows me to the bar, and Alex joins us. He has a friend with him, and they're heading out. On their way out, they pass the photographer from *The Star*, who asks if he can take a picture of Alex.

Our friend refuses. It wouldn't do for a middle grade fiction author to be photographed at a kinky art show.

Echoes of Luke, not wanting the Preston name attached to the show.

And yet now he waves the photographer over, introduces himself, and is happy to pose for a whole set of pictures with me.

BY THE TIME the show winds down, my cheeks hurt, my heart aches, and my feet are ready to fall off.

Luke drives me home, and I don't complain. Then he walks me to my door, which I also don't hate. When I unlock the door, he leans against the wall instead of heading for the elevator as he has the last couple of days. I give me a narrowed-eye *what are you doing* look.

He grins. "I'm going. I just want to make sure you get inside safely first."

I laugh and push the door open, but then the chuckle dies.

The loft is full of balloons, and there's a bottle of champagne sitting in an ice bucket just inside the door. Beside it is a newspaper, but when I step inside and pick it up, I realize it's today's paper with stuff glued to the front.

He's made a headline from other words and pasted over the real headline. The cobbled together one reads, ***Local Artist Stuns City With Incredible Show.***

The photo below it is a picture of me in my studio, which he must have printed from my website.

It's very thoughtful.

"One day you will be front page news. Canada's own dirty Banksy, and I'll remember tonight as that turning point. I'm not the artist that you are, but I did my best to capture—"

I spin around and throw my arms around him, cutting him off. "It's great," I mumble into his chest. "Thank you."

"Step by step," he whispers.

I twirl forward, grabbing some of the balloons, letting myself just be happy for a minute. When I stop, he's picked up the bottle of wine. "Do you want me to open this for you?"

"Do you want to share it?"

"Yes." Another grin. I've missed his smile. "But if you want me to leave you alone with it, that's fine too. Pour yourself a glass and go have a bubble bath."

That sounds nice, but company sounds better. "No. I want you to stay." I glance around the loft. He let himself in here earlier, which is…a problem. But a sweet one, and I'll worry about that tomorrow. "Stay here. I'll get glasses."

"We could move to the couch," he calls after me.

"Don't be so familiar," I holler back.

I grab two flutes and return, plopping myself down on the floor.

He joins me.

"Can we just sit together? Be still together?"

He nods.

"I'm kind of scared of sitting in stillness. I always have been. It sounds like a fate worse than death. Like if I stop moving, stop worrying…" I shudder.

"What will happen?"

"Self-doubt. Panic? Self-recrimination."

"I'm familiar with all three. I call them the shame monster."

I look at him in surprise. "Really?"

"Therapy."

That'll do it.

"How's the stillness going now?"

"We're still talking," I point out.

He mimes zipping up his mouth. Then he pours the wine, and it's good. We make it almost to the end of the bottle, just sitting there together, sipping the bubbly.

"It's a bit of a bittersweet end to the day," I finally say.

"Yeah." He brushes his pinky finger against mine. "Is that what came out of the stillness for you?"

"Yeah." I make a face, then realize my eyes are wet. I swipe away the sad tears.

"I'm sorry I've broken everything so badly." The way his voice cracks, I know he's sitting with an even bigger helping of self-recrimination than I ever could.

I move my hand on top of his and squeeze his fingers. "Thanks for coming tonight."

"It really was incredible."

"Even *Death of a Marriage?*"

He makes a wounded noise that turns into a coughing laugh. And he nods. "Yes."

"I have a confession," I whisper, ignoring the fear wrapping its cold fingers around my heart.

He turns his head, his handsome face bare and soft and fragile.

For the first time in what feels like a lifetime, I don't want to hurt him. "I'm sorry," I breathe. "In advance."

"It's okay." He pokes his tongue at the corner of his mouth, being strong and brave in the way that only being truly vulnerable allowed one to be. "Whatever it is, I'll understand."

Was I there yet? I take a deep breath. "I've been going to Alex's kink club for the past year. It started as research."

Luke's expression doesn't change, but even in the dim lighting, I see his Adam's apple bob up and down, and then I hear a tortured inhale. "Oh?"

"It never crossed the kind of lines you crossed. It wasn't like that. I didn't want anyone else. But I started to explore my sexuality, and I never had any plans to tell you about it. Deep down I had resigned myself to the fact that at some point, we had fractured beyond repair. I didn't owe you an explanation of what I was doing."

"You didn't," he said softly. "I said it was okay, and I meant it. Thank you for telling me."

I nod.

But I'm not done.

I'm so scared it hurts, in my shoulders and down my arms. I'm holding myself so rigidly it's painful, but it's painful inside my chest, too.

Like I might break if I finish the confession.

Like I might shatter if I don't.

"I think I owe you that explanation now." My voice is soft, or small. Maybe both. *I was still, and this burbled up.* "Because I think our fractured thing is something I still value."

He exhales, roughly, and thumps his head back against the wall. "Thank Christ," he mutters.

And he hauls me into his lap.

I HOLD HER AGAINST ME, my sweet wife, my beautiful wild bird, as she shakes and cries softly. She's done a big, brave thing, after another big, brave thing, and I love her so much for all of it.

"I'm sorry," I murmur against her hair. I will forever be that. And then, because sorry isn't enough, and not what she needs, I dig deeper. "I'm curious, too. I want you to tell me more when you're ready."

"Later," she whispers.

I kiss the side of her head and hold her.

Later comes at the bottom of the bottle of champagne. We drink it while eating a charcuterie board I put in the fridge earlier.

Once she's eaten and is quite tipsy, she stretches out on the floor and pats the space next to her.

I'm not getting past the foyer of the loft tonight, I realize that, so the floor is perfect. I lie down on my back, and after a few long beats of silence she starts talking.

"It took me months to realize I wasn't going there for research anymore. In hindsight, it was silly how long it took me, but denial is powerful."

My lips quirk at that. "So I've heard."

"It made my art so much richer, too." I turn my head to the side so I can watch her in profile. The softness of her cheek, the firm point of her nose. The rise and fall of her whole body as she takes a breath and holds it.

Waiting.

Stillness.

And then she smiles, which is the most beautiful thing in the world, and she starts talking again. "I was so mad," she says softly, still smiling. That hurts, but it's a dull hurt. Progress. "When I realized you'd played at kink with someone else. It took me a long time to realize that playing at kink and being kinky aren't at all the same things."

I'm not sure if I'm supposed to just listen, but I agree. When she doesn't continue, I gruffly make an agreeing noise so she knows I'm on board.

That makes her smile more.

"It's so hard to explain, actually." She snaps her fingers in the air. "Oh! Maybe..." She rolls onto her side, so we're looking at each other. "I want you to take a quiz."

Do I look like someone who can be defined by the interns at Cosmopolitan? The asshole response slams into my head, onto my tongue, before I can turn off the negativity. But I stop it from slipping out, and that's something. "Sure."

But she catches my hesitation. "Never mind."

"Grace, it's fine."

"No, it's really not. Either you want to do what it takes to fix this marriage or you don't."

"I do." That comes out immediately, no stopping it, and I exhale roughly. "Please. Tell me about this quiz."

"Maybe later." She twists away and jumps up, padding barefoot toward the kitchen. "I need a drink."

At this rate, we're going to be alcoholics before she likes me again. "Hey, wait."

She scowls at me over her shoulder. "Don't try to stop me."

"Can I at least follow you?"

She doesn't say no, so I haul myself up and follow anyway, bringing the empty champagne bottle and flutes with me.

She takes two glasses out of the cupboard, then points wordlessly at the liquor cabinet.

I hand her the scotch. She holds the bottle in her hand for a minute, then sets it down, turns again—always twisting away from me, like she can't look at me—and presses up onto her tiptoes to grab the vodka instead.

I follow the curve of her bare arm to the black silk of her shirt, stretching against her slight breasts, and suddenly I'm hard.

I want to fuck my wife against the kitchen counter.

I want to drag her to the floor and make her scream.

"What are you thinking?" she asks as she turns away from me again.

How does she know I'm thinking anything when she won't

even look at me? "I was thinking you look really hot right now."

"Stop being surprised I'm attractive, Luke."

"I'm never—" But maybe I am. "If I have been remiss in telling you how gorgeous you are, I will rectify that."

She snorts. "I know I'm pretty. That's not what I'm talking about." She lifts her glass to her lips and tips it back, swallowing the neat vodka in three slow pulses of her throat.

"No," I say hoarsely. "I know."

She turns and looks at me for the first time since she headed for the kitchen. "Do you?"

"You're a fucking sex kitten, and I lost sight of that for a while."

She wipes an errant drop of vodka from the corner of her mouth. "Exactly."

"I want you so much it hurts." My confession rips from my chest, and I gesture to the erection throbbing against the front of my dress pants. "Feel for yourself if you don't believe me."

Her eyes glint dangerously. "Do you think sex will fix what's broken between us?"

No. "Tell me about the quiz you want me to take."

"Maybe another time." She reaches for the bottle again. "One more drink before bed."

"What do you want tonight?"

Her gaze falls from my face, dragging down my body. "I don't know."

My cock presses obscenely against my fly, aching for more than just her doubting eyes. "Anything, baby."

She jerks her head up. "Don't call me that."

"Okay."

"You called her Kitten. Capital K."

"I told you—"

"You told me lies. You told me bullshit lies that maybe you also told yourself, because maybe you didn't want to be her Master for real, capital M, but you were, at least to her. In those moments, you were." Her voice is hard now, sharp and pointed. "And I don't want to be a lower-case anything to you, do you get that? I want a fucking capital letter. That's what I want."

She slams back another shot of vodka, then swings past me.

My glass is still sitting on the counter, untouched.

"You know what I did this morning, *Luke?*" She exhales sadly. "I went to the sexual health clinic to make sure that I don't have any infections because you brought someone else into our marriage bed without telling me. You don't have any right to stand in my kitchen and try to make this about sex."

"You brought up kink," I point out. I'm stupid, though.

"That's not about *sex,*" she snaps. "That's who I *am*. You don't get it."

"Then help me understand. Because I know I've fucked up, but it is *not* true if you think that someone I…used…for my own pathetic purposes is in any way comparable to you. You're *Mine*. That has a capital letter. The only one that has ever mattered to me, as much as I fucked up and lost sight of it. Nothing that I ever did with her mattered in the least. It was disposable and stupid."

"That's not a name. Mine. That's a possessive feeling, and probably misplaced."

"Names come in time. With trust. I haven't earned that yet."

She flicks her gaze away, locking on a distant point on the ceiling. "Maybe."

I swallow hard. "I have names that I've called you, and only you. In my mind."

She doesn't move. Doesn't breathe.

My heart pounds and my palms are slick with sweat, but I push through the panic. *Maybe she won't like it.* Well, she doesn't like me much as it is, anyway. Might as well burn the house down to find out what's in the ashes. "Baby girl. Little slut."

She gasps and her eyes dart toward me before she can stop herself. Her gaze is wide and bright. Shocked.

"It's not like I want you to call me Daddy or something," I add desperately. "But I guess, deep down, some of that kinky shit has always been there."

Her face tightens. "Got it. And you played that out with *her.*"

"No. It wasn't like that. She brought up the words she liked, and I rolled with it. But it was just regular sex. God, I'm not a monster. And I swear to God—"

She blanches. "No? Just a lying pig, then? Got it. Go away."

"Let's not end tonight like this. Please." I take a deep breath. "Look, I'm going to go, because we've had a lot to drink, and I don't want to make you more mad. But what I said…please think about it. Everything you want? I want that, too. With you. Only with you. And I want to figure out more about that together."

THE FIRST THING I do when I wake up is look up the sexual health clinic. It opens in an hour.

I'm waiting when they unlock the doors.

It's not unlike my therapy sessions. Cool, clinical assessment. I cheated on my wife. I don't know if my other partner had multiple partners herself. I think she did. Yes, we used condoms. And then the rush of shame. No, not every time.

When was the last time I had sex? Five weeks ago. I'll have to come back for a repeat test in a few months.

I nod through it all.

"Has your wife been tested?"

"Yes. She told me she did, so I thought...that's why I'm here."

"If you have sex again in the next two months, or any time with a non-monogamous partner, you should use barrier protection."

Numbly, I nod and take the handout with the phone number to call for results.

On my way back to the apartment, Grace texts.

Grace: Can we talk?

I text her that I'm five minutes away, and when I arrive,

she's waiting next to my door. She looks small and fragile, although it would be a mistake to ever think that about Grace.

She's the strongest woman I've ever known.

The most beautiful.

Too strong, too beautiful.

How did I let this happen? Regret clogs my throat. The last thing I need to do now is fall apart.

I need to be stronger for her. I need to be a fucking machine of hope.

"Come on in," I say, unlocking the door.

She follows me inside, and then gestures to the couch. "Maybe you should sit."

I do as I'm told.

"I thought about not telling you this," she says slowly. "Because…reasons. But then I realized I don't have anything to lose here."

My pulse hammers heavy in my neck. No, I'm the one who has everything to lose. "You can tell me anything."

"Can I?" Her eyes light up, bright and mean. Except Grace is never cruel. So if she's feeling sharp, if she's readying for battle, it's because I've hurt her.

I turn my hands over, palms up, and lean forward, trying to show her in every part of my body language that I want to hear whatever she has to say. "Anything. If I've hurt you—"

"If?"

I sigh. "I mean specifically with regards to this important thing."

"It's all specific, Luke. It's all—" She lets out a hollow laugh. "This is a mistake."

"No. Tell me. Anything. Please." I move to stand, but she flinches.

I'm so much bigger than her. Stronger, taller, wider, and now she sees all of that as a threat.

I sit again, agony ripping my throat out. What else can I say?

Nothing.

She glares at me. She might think that's being mean, that's hurting me, but it doesn't. I love the heat of her gaze, the hard push against my skin. As long as she's looking at me, hating me, I know she still loves me. Deep down, I'm hers, and she hates me for taking some of that from her, but she knows I can give it back.

"I don't know how much you know about kink," she says coolly. "And now you know that I am...familiar...with that world. Only artistically, only to the research level, but I've read a lot. Taken classes at The Wheelhouse."

"You know more than me," I admit hoarsely. "A lot more. It wasn't...I never thought of myself as kinky. I was going along with it."

Her lips pull tight, and the faint smile doesn't reach her eyes. "And now?"

"Now what?"

"Now are you starting to realize some of those things are deep down? Is that what you meant when you shared...what you think of me?"

Baby girl. Little slut.

I guess I showed my hand more than I realized. "Sure. Yeah."

"When you said it's not like you want me to call you Daddy, that hurt me." She licks her lips as a dull roar starts to churn in my ears. "The thing is, that's one fantasy that's always been consistently hot for me. It's why I wanted you to take that quiz I found."

"The quiz is about kink?" Fuck. I clench my fists, trying hard to focus on what she's saying. But all I can hear is her sweet little voice echoing in my head. *Daddy. Fantasy. Daddy. Fantasy.* "Shit, Grace, if you have a Daddy fantasy, that's okay."

She flinches. "I know it's okay."

"Do you?" I rise out of my chair, my heart pounding. "Don't look at me like that. It's fine." It's more than fine. Fuck. "That's…interesting, actually. I want to know more about that." *I want to know more about you, my mysterious little wife.*

"You didn't want to know more about me wanting to be spanked, and that's something a lot of people do. Often people who use words like *Daddy* and *Baby Girl.*"

"I wasn't listening then. I'm listening now. I'm here. I'm present. Tell me." Desperate pleas fill my brain, gag me in their need to spill out, but I can't overwhelm her. *Please, fuck, tell me. Tell me everything, and I will love it. I love you so much.* I choke all of those thoughts back and wait. Listening.

"There's a part of me—last night, for example—that wants you to take this quiz, figure out your kink preferences, and then we could start over again. Maybe. Down the road. But there's another part of me that is worried, deeply, that whatever you are feeling for me now is temporary. The attraction that you feel for me doesn't feel real." She takes a deep breath. "I told you that I know her name. I've looked her up online. I know she's pretty. Younger than me, sexier than me—"

"No."

"Yes." Her voice cracks. "Because remember that I also know what it is to be the wife you don't see. To be a woman, changing in front of her husband, knowing he couldn't care less. When I remember those moments, I feel hopelessly unattractive. I worry that your new attraction to me is desperate and responsive, not organic. And I know you don't like hearing that, don't want me to say that. I can see it on your face right now, you want to protest."

I do. That's not how it feels for me at all, but I can't argue with her, either.

And then she says the worst thing, because it's ugly and it's true. "Until I found out about your affair, you really struggled with how you felt about my body."

Fuck.

"That was—I've talked to my therapist about that—" I know I should just keep quiet. "But it's not exactly right. Think about all the good times we had. Remember when—"

"I remember," she says smoothly. Her eyes are deep, endless pools of sorrow. "I'm just providing some context. I know we had some good times, too."

"I don't like that you feel this way." I shove my hand in my hair. "I wish I could take away those feelings."

"You can't. Because me finding out about the affair, it was like a switch was flipped, and you realized that way of thinking hadn't done you any favours."

"I did realize that. Yes, exactly. It was shame, and grandiosity, and—" I stop myself.

She gives me a small smile I don't deserve. "So you tackled that as something to fix. But you haven't ever dealt with the fact that our marriage was built on that. That can't be fixed or undone."

"I'm not going to deny the past. Maybe repair isn't the right objective. Maybe we should try to start over. And now isn't the time. I went to the sexual health clinic today. After you said that last night, when I woke up, I looked into it, and went as soon as they opened. They told me I should be tested again in a few months. So let's wait that long. I'll be celibate for as long as it takes, to prove to you I'm serious about this."

"And why should I be celibate that long?" She crosses her arms.

It's the second time she's brought up dating.

And with a newfound horror, I realize what I need to do to win my wife back. I need to truly let her go.

21

GRACE

To his credit, Luke stops interrupting me, and listens to everything I have to say. We don't fight, we just talk, and when I leave his apartment, he says he needs some time to think, and he wants to come over for tea later this afternoon.

After I leave his apartment, I go to the gallery because it makes me happy. I walk, because it's a glorious day, sunny and bright, and on the return walk home, I call Hazel.

"Hello?"

"Hi Hazel, it's Grace."

"Oh, hey." She murmurs my name. "Sam says hi."

I laugh. "I wanted to follow up on last night. I really would like to get coffee. How long are you in the city?"

"A few days. How does tomorrow sound?"

"Like a date. I'll come to you."

We set a time, and I end the call just before letting myself into my building.

What an absolutely lovely, normal afternoon. It feels like

I've finally exhaled, after holding my breath for weeks. I've said everything I need to say to Luke, I'm back on track with work, and my life can begin moving forward again.

Upstairs, I put the kettle on and text Luke that I'm home whenever he wants to chat again.

At this rate, I might not even need therapy for myself. We're actually figuring out a way through this. Maybe we'll be amicably divorced by the summer.

It's a strange thought. Makes me feel a little empty, and I'm still contemplating that when his knock sounds at the door.

I let him in, and this is immediately a different man than I left in his apartment this morning. He's done something, I can tell. "What's going on?"

"Now it's your turn to sit," he says grimly.

"You're scaring me." The kettle whistles, and I hold up a finger. "Wait a second."

I pour water into the teapot, then leave it. Something tells me I don't need to entertain him right now. I stalk back into the living room and curl up on the armchair, because he's sitting on the couch. "What is it?"

"Everything you said this morning…I heard all of it. I don't want you to live with any kind of doubt, and I need to fully own the damage I have done. The truth is, I collapsed in on myself just as much as our firm did. In a time of acute crisis, I failed to do the right thing on every level. Looking back, I see that I just abdicated my responsibility to this marriage. To you. I won't make the same mistake again."

There's a real resignation to his voice, and it alarms me,

even though he's saying everything I want to hear. "What are you doing?"

"The right thing, no matter how much I hate it." He hands over a printed piece of paper. "I've written something I want you to read."

I reach out and take it.

I have to read it twice to understand what it is saying.

To Whom It May Concern, So Long As You Are a Better Person Than I Am;

I want you to date my wife. See, the thing is, I cheated on her. Like a lot of cheating spouses, I don't have any good reasons why I did it. Sex, escape, adrenaline.

But I didn't do it out of any sense of romance or love. Those, as pathetic as it sounds, are reserved for my wife, and she doesn't want them from me right now.

So I think you should give it a go.

Know that I will always want her. Know that I will always love her. But I think she deserves a chance at a selfless love that doesn't ask as much as my love asks.

Let me tell you about her. She's creative as hell. Smart. Gorgeous. Her beauty is quiet, but lasting. She's prettier now than she was when we met in university, although she was the most beautiful woman I had ever seen then, and still is. She's sexier now, too, in ways I was too selfish to properly explore when I had the chance. She works with

her hands, with her entire body, and it shows. She's got softness, too.

The way her muscles move beneath her curves is the most erotic thing I can picture.

Now she deserves the chance to freely be who she wants to be without any pressure.

If you think you might be the right person to give this woman the happiness she deserves—for a night, a day, a week, a month, or forever—submit your best effort to the P.O. Box listed below. All submissions will be treated with the utmost confidence by the person with the most integrity of anyone I've ever known.

My wife.

Who I don't deserve.

I won't know the entries. I've given her the key to the P.O. Box, and she won't share them with me. She won't want to, and that has to be my cross to bear.

"You're joking," I whisper.

"No."

"Luke, this is a hell of a way to tell me that I'm pretty."

"That's not what I'm doing. You are, by the way. Very pretty."

"You want me to date other people? Through a system *you* have set up, rather than just, you know, the normal way."

"You don't need to use the letter if you don't want to." He shrugs, his whole body tight. "I just thought—I mean, it's mostly for you, so you know how I feel about you. Yeah, that's true. But I'm serious about other people dating you. You dating…other people. That's—you should have that. If you want it."

"And what if I say I do?" I stand up, furious and desperately in need of a cup of tea to restore me to the perfectly reasonable day I had been having up until he gave me this note. "Don't answer that."

I wish I was only angry. Sadness is a bigger emotion. Takes up more space. Lasts a hell of a lot longer.

I fill the largest mug I own, a handmade thing Luke gave me one year for Christmas that has a chip in it, but I keep because it's my favourite—and oh, the irony is not lost on me there—and take my time adding milk and sugar.

The last thing I want is my cheating husband to pimp me out to strangers out of some sense of obligation.

The way her muscles move beneath her curves is the most erotic thing I can picture.

What the fuck is that? He has no right to describe me like that. Not anymore.

I take a steadying breath, pick up my mug, and return to the living room. He hasn't changed positions at all.

It's such a strange idea to consider as I sit across from him, drinking tea out of a mug he gave me, in the loft I bought us to rebuild our lives after his firm almost imploded.

But maybe he's right. Maybe I need to test this out. If we're going to come to an end anyway, why not rip that bandaid off sooner than later?

"You're serious," I repeat for what feels like the tenth time.

"What's the saying? If you love something, set it free."

My heart pounds in my chest. "And what if I'm not ready to start dating?"

"It's up to you. But if you ever want a reference letter for a—"

"Shut up." I close my eyes and breathe in the scent of tea. Think about the shape of the mug in my hand, the sounds of Luke being in my apartment again.

And I imagine everything being different.

Different men, different mugs.

22

GRACE

It takes me two weeks to realize that Luke is serious about this. We both get the all clear from the health clinic, which is a relief.

I don't like the idea of him posting that ad about me, although I keep the printout of his letter in my bedside drawer. There's something deeply kinky about it, and I can't put my finger on it exactly—but the only place I would consider playing with something like that is The Wheelhouse, and with both Sam and Alex connected to that space, it's a non-starter for using it to have some side fun outside of my marriage.

Even if it is officially sanctioned by my husband.

The idea of it makes me hot and achy, but…no.

I do like *the idea*, though. But in reality, I'm not that kind of woman. I'm pretty sure.

And then something happens that drags me back into the muck, into the despair and the grossness of infidelity.

I get a phone call from a woman who tracked me down through the gallery.

"You don't know me," the woman says, her voice breaking. "But I think we both have a problem with Caitlyn Jobst."

My stomach drops away, like an endless dark chasm has opened up inside me. I start shaking. "Yes, I know her. Sort of. I mean—"

"My husband just left me. I think they've been having an affair. And you had responded to some of his pictures last month…"

I remember now. "I was drunk," I whisper. "And drunk and Facebook don't really work well together. I'm sorry."

"Don't be sorry. It started something…I asked him about it. He didn't know who you were, but he got shifty when I asked him about Caitlyn."

"She had an affair with my husband, too. I know of one other affair as well. It's her thing."

There's a long pause. "Did he leave you?"

My heart cracks open. I don't know if this answer is better or worse. Like everything else in this fucked up story, it is what it is. "It's complicated. I asked him to leave. We're trying to work on it, maybe, but I dunno."

"Oh."

Yeah, oh. That's accurate. "I'm so sorry."

"I know it's his fault," she says. Like I did.

Like I'm sure we all do, and the thing is, it *is* his fault. Our partners are absolutely to blame for the fuckery they bring to our lives.

But at what point can you point to a serial home-wrecker

and say, she's a fucking problem, too? What dark trauma did she suffer as a child that made her grow up to want to destroy the happiness of other women?

Or maybe it's the men. Maybe she has twisted Daddy issues. Maybe she wants to hurt them and ruin their lives, and we're an inconsequential side effect.

I don't fucking care anymore.

I do care about this woman, though. I think she's fucking brave to reach out to me. I care about being present and hearing her story. "Do you want to grab some coffee and talk?"

"If you have time."

"I have all the time in the world." I was supposed to go for a walk with Luke. Cancelling is the no-brainer choice.

Grace: Something's come up. I'll talk to you tomorrow.
Luke: Okay. I love you.
Grace: I know.

And I do. But right now, I don't care.

There is a brutal double standard for women who have been cheated on. On the hand, they are blamed for it. They weren't sexy enough, they ignored their husband's needs. And then, when they find out, they are expected to leave.

You think people are rewarded for staying with a spouse that betrayed them? Not by people who see them as having agency. Agency means we leave. Period. Agency means, when I'm hurt, I run.

I'm not exactly running. But I feel pretty fucking lonely in this place of fighting for what I want. Like he can't possibly love me if he's hurt me. Like he never loved me, not really, and so I should give him up because he wasn't good enough for me.

But there's a part of me that doesn't want to give him up. I've loved him this whole time. We had a really wonderful life until it fell apart. I want that back. But better this time. I don't want to try to find that with someone else, either.

I could have it now.

So why does it feel so precarious?

Will it ever not feel this precarious?

And why, as I head out the door to meet another wronged woman, are my thoughts tangled up in trying to redeem Luke?

Fuck him.

Fuck Caitlyn, too.

LUKE

GRACE IS mad in a new way, an incandescent way, when she shows up on my doorstep.

She's also dressed for sex again, and I notice. I can't *not* notice, even if I'm supposed to be letting her go. She's got a short, swingy skirt on. Easy access. And a halter top that promises she's not wearing a bra.

I want to grab her. Pin her down.

"Come on in," I say instead, playing at being civilized. "I thought from your text…"

"Your girlfriend has now wrecked a second marriage in less than a month," she spits at me.

I rock back on my heels.

"Another wife found me. It pays to have a public face, I guess."

"How did she connect you to…?"

Grace waves her hand. "That doesn't matter."

I bet it does. "Uh huh."

"But the point is, your little affair wasn't as benign as you think it was."

"I don't think it was benign. I think I fucked everything up, and I've tried to be as honest about that as I can."

Another wave.

Okay. We're not interested in what I have to say, and that's fine. It's not fucking great, but apparently the grief cycle of infidelity is a rollercoaster you didn't ask to be strapped into, and all I can do now is hold on for dear life.

A mistake of my own making, Grace would rightly point out.

"She decided, over and over again, to fuck married men. Did you know that?"

"I don't know. No."

"You weren't the only one."

"I guess I wasn't."

"You weren't the only one to have secrets with her, to be all the little things his wife was not. She was that to *other* men, too. That's fucked up, right?"

"Yes. I guess so. I don't think about her anymore."

"I wish I had that privilege. So she's moved on to another married man now. And this one doesn't seem to care about hurting his wife in public. Should I be grateful that at least I don't have to deal with the humiliation out there, as well as in here?"

"How did she *know to find you*, Grace?" I'm yelling a little now. Fuck me. I take a deep breath. "Look, I'm sorry for that woman. I am. But you've let someone else's drama pull you into a tailspin here."

"It's not fucking fair," she spits at me, shoving me in the chest.

I catch her by the wrist and pull her onto the couch. "I know."

She exhales roughly. "I'm angry."

"I know." I twist a lock of her hair around my finger and tug gently. I yearn for the same fairytale she does, but it's not realistic.

She grabs my wrist, stopping me from touching her hair. But then she pulls my touch to her breast and we both gasp.

"No," I groan, but I don't mean it. Still, I try to be better than this. Moving my hands to her shoulders, then her hips, I pull her close. Pretend it's just a hug. It doesn't matter that she's angry. I still love her just as much. If anything, her anger helps. It gives me some direction for the darkness inside. Some form, a clear penance, for the yawning grossness that would otherwise be overwhelming. "Be angry. Be loud. Be whatever you need to be. I'm right here and I'm not going anywhere."

"I don't like this." She climbs into my lap and I'm helpless to say no. Her skirt rides up high on her thighs.

The warmth of her body scrambles my brain, and when I lift my hand to her arms, where I can touch her and bring her in close, I feel goosebumps rise on her skin. First the delicate, soft, pale blonde whispers of hair on her arms lift. I'm frozen, barely touching her.

Then the gooseflesh comes, a ripple of nerves, and I sink

my fingers into her skin. It's just me but that's wrong, because I'm the devil to her. I'm dangerous.

And she sighs.

"We shouldn't..." I don't bother finishing that thought. I want to, is the problem.

She licks her lips. "I want to do something tonight."

"Anything." As long as I can hold her.

"I want to go out for dinner. Someplace kind of wild and loud."

"Deal." I will make this happen for her. I will fill her day with noise and delight and spoilage the likes of which she's never had before, so she doesn't have to feel the anger which is completely justified—but which she hates so much.

Anger at anger.

My beautiful wife. Too good for me by a mile. So good it hurts her to stay with me.

I don't deserve her love. I hold her tight anyway. "I love you so much," I tell her as she leans into me. Between us, my cock flexes.

She rocks against my erection.

"Careful," I warn her.

"I don't want to be careful." She pushes up, sitting squarely on my lap as she grinds away. "I want you to fill me up before we go out. I want to feel your come slick on my thighs as we—"

I shove my hands under her skirt, gripping her hips tight. What I want to do is rip her panties to the side and shove two fingers deep into her cunt. "Dangerous game."

She smiles. "Fuck me."

I twist her around, so she's flat on her back on the couch. "No. Not yet."

"Not until I've dated other people?"

"Maybe." I stroke the front of her thighs. Right along the edge of her panties.

"It's okay," she whispers. "I just want to rub against you."

Need pools low inside me, her murmured words conjuring a filthy fantasy I can't fully admit. Forbidden, dangerous thoughts that make me a bad man. She sounds so fucking innocent, a siren-by-accident. An unknowing temptress who will find herself full of cock before she knows it.

But this is Grace.

She *does* know it. She's a sex connoisseur, and she's tapped into something here.

"We can't have sex," I mutter again.

Her voice goes soft and dreamy. "I know." Then she rolls her hips. "Is this okay?"

"Does it feel good?"

"Mmm hmm."

"You can rub against me, as long as it feels good." I'm going to hell. I roll us around so I'm on the bottom and she's perched on top of me. I stroke her back with my fingertips. "Be a good girl for me and figure out what feels good."

She mewls at that, a horny, wild sound I've never heard before, and her thighs clench down on my hips. Slowly, she rocks against my erection, and I whisper filth into her ear.

"There are two ways it can feel good. You have a perfect, wet little hole that wants a cock in it, and that will feel nice, if you rub that opening against my cock. Mmm. See how hard I get when you do that? That makes me want to do bad things to you. But I won't. We can't. You need to keep your panties on, okay?"

"Mmm hmm." She shudders. "Oh, this feels so good."

I drift my hands lower, to cup her ass and adjust her angle a little. "And there's another spot you can rub against me."

"My clit," she whispers. "I like that spot. I touch it at night."

Now it's my turn to make feral, ungodly sounds. "Tell me about that."

"That's how I get to sleep at night. I rub my clit with two fingers, around and around, and think about bad men who call themselves Daddy touching me under the covers."

Her words slide into my brain and push on live wires I have never consciously allowed myself to connect before. "Grace…" I gasp as she rocks her hips. "Yes. Fuck. Rub against me."

She presses her face into my neck, her breath hot against my skin, and I jerk my hips, desperate to come with her, wishing we weren't closed, wishing I knew how to do this without hurting, wishing I was touching her under a blanket and making her come on my fingers first, then my cock.

"You can always ask me for this," I settle on, my voice cracking as her breath quickens, her hips flying now. "This is safe. This is just for us. Nobody else will ever know that we like this. God, you feel good. Yes. Come for me. Come on Daddy's cock, Grace. Do it. Fuck. Fuck, you're so little, so perfect, so hot, fuck I'm coming Grace…"

"Do you still want dinner?"

She looks at me wide-eyed. "Uh…"

"Fuck, was that too far?"

"No." She whispers it. A single sound. Then she shakes her head. "That was hot."

"I didn't think—"

"I started it." She kisses me, quickly, then glances down at my crotch. "Do you need to clean up?"

"Yeah." Which is easier said than done in a single room loft. I get my, my pants a sticky disaster, and ignore that the best I can as I grab a change of clothes from the suitcase on the floor. Then I toss them on the bed, because fuck it, she's my fucking wife, and I cross to the bathroom instead.

Leaving the door open as I strip out of my clothes, I wet a washcloth and scrub jizz off my belly. Then I stalk back to the bed and pull on boxers and fresh jeans. Good enough for now.

"You're freaking out," she finally says.

I shrug.

"It's okay, Luke. It was just sex."

That was not *just* anything. "Mmm hmmm."

"Look at me." She says it softly, and I blink down at her. She has a smile that matches the tone of her voice. Gentle.

I don't want gentle, I want safe.

Maybe for the first time, I get the difference. She's being gentle as fuck with me, but this doesn't feel safe at all. "Those things I said…"

"Were fine. And hot. And what I needed to get off in a pretty spectacular way." She stands and adjusts her halter top. "Now to answer your question, yes, I do still want dinner, but I'm going to have to change first, because there's no way I'm leaving the building like this."

24

GRACE

WE DON'T DO it again. I don't know why. I don't feel like seducing him again, probably, and he doesn't initiate it, which irritates me for reasons I know I have no right to be irritated by. So after another week, I decide, fuck it, I'm going to try his dating plan.

Not with the P.O. Box. Nobody needs to know my husband is still pining for me, that's weird. Not to me, it's secretly starting to feel very sweet to me in a dangerous way, but it would be weird to anyone outside our relationship.

Instead, I download a couple of apps, and try my hand at internet flirting with strangers.

It's not fun at all.

The first date is a non-event, a complete disaster of nothingness. I show up, I order a drink at the bar, and I people watch. No sign of the guy who I emailed back and forth with a bit. Nobody who looks anything like his picture. He finally arrives ten minutes after the hour, and it's awkward and painful.

I give him twenty minutes, then my phone rings. It's actually an alarm I set, but he can't see my screen and doesn't know that. I turn off the alarm, pretend to answer a call, and get the hell out of there.

On my way home, I pick up a bottle of expensive red wine and a takeout order of lobster mac and cheese. While it heats in my oven, I have a shower and wash off the failure of my first date in eighteen years, and think about all the reasons why I can't just send Luke a picture of me in pigtails and see what happens.

At nine o'clock, I send a mean text message to Luke. Mean, because I purposefully leave a lot of doubt as to how my evening is going.

It feels good.

Grace: Had my first date tonight.

It takes him a few minutes to reply.

Luke: Okay.

Jackass. This was his idea. I don't care if he doesn't like it. Actually, I care a great deal. I don't want him to like it.

I put my phone on do not disturb mode and flip to Tumblr. I'm having sex tonight, even if it's just by myself. I'm going to have a lot of sex tonight.

Red wine and lobster fuelled sex, so it's probably going to be weird.

THE SECOND DATE is five days later. This one smells good. A little spicy and warm. He smells like a stranger. He smells exciting. And when he touches me on the arm, guiding me from the bar to our table, it feels good. It feels a little wrong, too, but mostly it feels good.

This is a secret pleasure that's just for me. From the first inhale of his peppery cologne, I knew this date would only be one night, but it might be a very good night.

And so I shake off every fear I can't quite name, and revel in how good it feels to have big rough hands touch me. He's handsy, this guy. Likes to touch my fingers across the table, bump his leg against mine.

After dinner, we take a walk, and before I get in the cab, he kisses me good night in a way that makes my thighs shake.

When I get home, I text Luke again.

Grace: Second date.
Luke: Same guy?
Grace: No.
Luke: Good.

IT ISN'T until I'm getting ready for the third date that I realize my variation of Luke's plan doesn't actually work. This guy's name is Javi, and he's a military pilot. He's not in the city that often, doesn't live here, but he's looking for a hook-up.

And I am not.

I'm pretending that I am, but that's a lie I'm telling myself, because as fun as these dates are, they don't hold a candle to what Luke and I did on his couch.

Fuck.

If I'm going to try dating, I actually need to have sex with one of these guys, and Javi seems like a good enough option.

And then, at the last second, he cancels. Work, he says.

Sure, I bet.

And so I quietly shelve the dating plan. I don't tell Luke about it. He doesn't ask. And another week rolls by. The days are warmer now, we're well into spring, and the whole city is starting to bloom.

I still feel like I'm covered in a layer of permafrost, but I'm not tempted to try the dating apps again.

And then one night, my phone vibrates. Three messages, sent back to back.

Javi: Hey, sorry for the radio silence, but I was away for work and spotty reception.

Javi: Legit spotty. I was in Resolute Bay.

Javi: But I'm back in Toronto for the weekend, and I'm interested in meeting up for a coffee sometime. Any time, really.

I grin like an idiot.

Grace: Where are you right now? I'm downtown.
Javi: I can be there in thirty minutes.

JAVI IS NICE. And hot. And after two cups of coffee, I'm not tired at all.

"Do you want to take a walk?"

"Sure."

He stands first, coming around to pull out my chair for me.

I like the way he smells. I like the way his fingers brush ever so gently against my back, then fall away again.

"So you were way up north," I ask as we step outside. We talked about everything except his work while we drank coffee.

"Yep."

And maybe we won't talk about it now, either.

That's fine. I'm not looking for his life story.

"How long are you in the city now?"

"Just the weekend. Then I'm going to Trenton for a while."

"Cool."

"Nice to have someone to hang out with a bit before I go, though." Clear boundaries. He's not looking for a relationship.

That's fine.

I'm only looking for one night. "I'm kind of busy with

work, and some personal stuff," I say. "But I'm giving myself tonight to just be…free."

"Free is good."

"Free is very good." I wink at him. "Do you want to go back to your place?"

"My place is a hotel room at the Marriott. Does that work?"

It's perfect. "Sure. Let me just text a friend and tell them where I'm going."

I hesitate for a second before I tap the message out. I know it's probably across the line.

Grace: Another date tonight. Might be out all night. I'm at the Marriott.

Luke: Understood. Be safe.

I shove my phone into my purse and take Javi's hand.

25

GRACE

I TEXT Luke the next morning and he doesn't reply, so I go downstairs.

He answers the door, eventually, looking hungover in the worst way. He's barely got a grasp on a glass of water. He doesn't say anything, just steps back, letting me in, and my heart sinks.

How do I explain what I'm thinking? How I feel? I grab the glass from his and take a desperate gulp—

"That's not water," Luke says as I gasp and choke against the unexpected burning tingle.

"What the fuck are you drinking?"

"Tequila."

I blink at him through watery eyes. "At nine in the morning?"

"I didn't realize it had gotten that late."

I look at him again, more carefully this time.

He's not hungover. He's drunk. There's no way I can try to

have a calm, rational conversation with someone who is blitzed out of his mind. "Why didn't you say something?"

Shrugging, he sways to the couch. "Hardly seemed like there was time before you just stole my drink."

"You can't drink a water glass full of tequila at nine in the morning. Or any time." I set the glass down in his kitchenette and join him on the couch.

He gives me a sad look. "You were on dates."

I take a deep breath. "Which you told me to go on."

"And I meant that. But it was hard to picture."

"Welcome to my world."

"Yeah." He closes his eyes.

"I shouldn't have told you I was going on them."

Another shrug. "I deserve it."

"I'm done with all of that."

He freezes. Then, slowly, he blinks his eyes open and looks at me. "Why?"

"Because I know what I want now."

"I'm too drunk for this conversation, aren't I?"

"Probably." I shift closer. "Or maybe you're just drunk enough to tell me the truth about the Daddy thing."

He groans. "Oh, fuck."

"Did you ever do the Daddy/baby girl—"

"Never." He says it fast and sure, like the question sobered him up.

"I need you to take that quiz," I whisper. "Because it's not that simple for me. I took a whole class about being Little and I'm not really that, exactly."

"I'm definitely too drunk to know what that means, but there are classes?"

I nod. "There are."

"I have a lot to learn, don't I?"

"Yep."

He catches my hand and pulls it to his mouth. He kisses my knuckles, then gives me a sad look. "How are you sleeping?"

"I'm not." I bite my lower lip. "Do you remember what I said when we were fooling around? I need to masturbate like that to fall asleep."

His mouth falls open. I wonder if he'll remember that when he sobers up.

He moves his hand to my face and strokes my cheek. "I wish we had done a lot of things differently."

"Me too." Then I jump all the way in. "We still can."

He crushes his mouth against mine, claiming me, and I free fall into his embrace. He makes a noise, sweet and agonizing at the same time, and hoists me up. Drunk, but still strong.

I need more. I claw at his shirt, desperate for the feel of his skin under my fingers.

He changes the angle of the kiss, deepening it.

For years, everything felt hard, like the world wasn't turning properly on its axis. This isn't hard. I hate that and love it at the same time, but I'm done fighting it.

"I wrote you another note," he groans as I move my mouth down his neck.

"I'm done being offered to strangers on the street."

"Isnotthat," he mumbles. Then he gently shoves me off him and grabs a notepad at the end of the couch. On it are a bunch of lines, half-formed thoughts, and then three sentences are underlined.

Trust

Doubt

Faith

Evidence

I know you will always have a reason to doubt me.
I can't erase that.
But I want to give you more reasons to let me love you anyway.

He drops the notepad and grabs my hands. "I know I'm drunk. I really didn't like the idea of you going to a hotel, and what my brain did with that information. But doing things different, yeah. I like that plan. Tell me what you want. Maybe I want it, too? I do want it. I want everything Grace wants."

The list rolls off my tongue with ease. I know it inside and out by now. "I want to cook dinner with my partner almost every night. Side by side in the kitchen, sharing a bottle of wine. Half drunk on it by the time we eat, and the things that we eat…I want pasta, without a care in the world for whether it bloats me. I want all the fucking bread. I want fancy salad and a big ass porterhouse for two. I want to make those decisions together, with someone who is as into food as I am, because he isn't hung up on what he looks like. I want—"

"Let me give that one a try. The food. And I want to share a bottle of wine with you."

"You don't like wine."

"That was the old me. Obviously I can drink tequila, which tastes like a cactus fell into a vat of vodka, so let me give wine a chance."

"Maybe no booze at all would be smarter," I whisper. But when have I ever been smart? "I went on a bit of a rant about the food, but that's just the start of the list."

"Let me make dinner with you tonight," he says, his voice urgent. "And you give me the rest of the list as we cook together."

26

LUKE

She leaves me to sleep off the tequila, and when I wake up in the early afternoon, there's a text message from her.

Fear grips my chest as I click into it, fully expecting her to have cancelled our plans. Instead, she's given me an instruction.

Grace: I want to try making cacio e pepe. Can you go shopping?
Grace: And how's your head?

Fingers shaking, I type back an affirmative response.

Luke: Shopping, yep. And the head will survive, but no more tequila for a while.

Then I google whatever the fuck *cacio e pepe* is, find out it's some glorified Mac and cheese, and tell myself it's literally, truly the least I can fucking do.

I remain an absolute bastard, though, because it's not until I've read three recipes on it that I'm even remotely interested in this. It sounds like a coma-inducing carb nightmare.

I couldn't be more wrong.

GRACE'S CHEEKS are pink from the steam, and she nudges my elbow. "Hurry, Luke," she says, her voice light with laughter. "You need to add the cheese now, and I'll stir."

I jostle around her, my arms long enough to bracket her as I grate the block of parmesan with the new rasp I bought just in case the one we've never used in our kitchen isn't sharp enough.

The pasta smells amazing. Peppery and salty, it's coming together into a dish that I guess I've seen her order in restaurants, but never really thought about.

We've made something here, together, and it's kind of fucking amazing.

"All right, I think that's good," she says, wiggling with joy. "Let me grab two bowls, and—"

She twists in the bracket of my arms and I turn us around, intending to point her in the direction of the cupboard where we keep the bowls, but she winds up clinging to me instead of spinning away.

She's pressed against me. She can feel I'm hard for her. Her breath comes shallow, sweet and panting, which only makes me throb more.

"Luke…"

"I'm enjoying making dinner together," I say, my voice low and rough. "Just ignore the rest of it."

"I'm not ready."

"I know." But that means she might be soon.

Time to learn how to cook a porterhouse for two. My wife wants variety? She wants a partner to bump into in the kitchen, until her cheeks are pink and my cock is aching for more than a scant brush against her body?

Fucking hell, I can be that guy.

I *am* that guy.

And I'm as surprised as she is.

We plate up our pasta, and she watches me with a funny look on her face as I light a candle for the table.

"A bit on the nose?"

She shakes her head. "I like it."

Good.

A plan is coming together, and after dinner, when she excuses herself to use the washroom, I have time to really sit in this space that she made for us and think about what my next step is.

If we're going to do this, it has to be completely new. It has to start in a completely different way.

I have to be a new and different man. For too long, I bought into the lie that you can't change a person. I just accepted that I was turning into my father as I got older. But the truth is, *that* was changing a person. I went from being a young man who was worthy of Grace to a middle-aged asshole she rightfully kicked to the curb.

I want to be the guy she fell in love with again. Without the baggage he was silently carrying. I want to be who she wanted to grow old with once upon a time. I want to be what she thought I could be. And to do that, I'm going to have to go back, strip myself of everything that I have learned over the last ten years, and undo all of the mistakes that I have made.

The poor choices I have made.

I need to get myself back to that pivotal moment when I stopped listening to my wife and I need to start listening, again.

I need to show her that I will do it as fast as I can. But also, because I'm serious about it, because I want this to be real and lasting and forever, that it won't happen overnight.

And I can show her that incremental work. I can be honest about my progress.

What about setbacks? My first reaction is denial. There won't be any setbacks, my grandiosity wants to claim, but that's not true.

And then there's the kink stuff, which fucking hell is so hot, but intense. She wants some sort of daddy figure, strong, and unwavering. How does that go hand in hand with a humble man who admits that he's failed miserably at keeping her safe?

The acid churn is back. And I don't like it. But what I like even less is that echo, that visceral body memory of how I ran from the challenge in the past.

I can't run from it now, I have to sit here and feel disgusted with myself and look at that shame and think, *you're not going to get the better of me today*. I'm going to stare at you, until you get smaller and turns into nothing.

"What are you thinking about?" She slides onto the couch beside me and curls up in the circle of my arms.

"You. And me. Mostly me, and how I want to be this perfect man."

"That's how you were raised."

"Pretty sure my nannies..." I trail off, not meaning to argue. "Right. The Preston way."

"It's not real, but that's part of the brainwashing, right? You were taught to always live a lie."

"I sure managed to excel at that." I roll my shoulders.

"Are you tense?" She climbs into my lap, an unconventional way to give a neck rub, but I'm not complaining. I spread my thighs wide to balance us and she strokes her hands up and down the side of my neck. "Tell me more."

"I want to be a better man for you. Unravel myself to the point where I went wrong, and fix it from there. Be the guy you wanted to grow old with. Remake myself in the original vision, but with less baggage. That's it in a nutshell, basically."

"That's all good stuff." She gives me a level look. "Can I ask about the affair? No shouting, no getting mad. I just... wanna know some things."

I nod. "Yes."

"Before we are intimate again," she laughs lightly. "That's so serious. Before we get carried away like we did last time, I really would like to negotiate some of the kinky elements specifically. I have a pretty complicated list of limits around the Little stuff, and some of them are common things in porn, so…"

The WASP in me is dying. The earnest husband, though, is all on board. "Okay. Yeah. I'm game for that."

"Did you do any of that limit negotiation with…her?"

I shake my head. "I'm going to keep telling you this. It wasn't like that. I was playing at something, and I didn't even understand the game. Now that I understand it, I'm glad that I've only really played the game for real with you. And it's not a game, I know that, it's who you really are, and I think that's beautiful."

She smiles, looking pleased, and I'm glad I got at least one answer right. I reach for something I talked about with my therapist. "That was nothing. Less than nothing. That was desperation. Cocaine off the back of a dirty toilet. A death spiral. It was grandiosity. Self-destruction. A form of addiction, probably. It could have been gambling or drugs. I took what was offered as a way to numb the pain of what I had done to myself. It was never real."

"Have you been in contact with her again?"

I shake my head. "No. Not since that night."

"And this is real? You and me?"

"Always. Forever. And it'll take time for you to believe that on enough levels that the pain I've caused is balanced out." I look at her, my sexy goddess, and need to know something. "Can I ask you, why did you decide to give me another chance?"

"Maybe for the same reason," she murmurs, her gaze searching my face. "For that young man I fell in love with in college. For the scared little boy he carried inside, for the way he protected his brother."

Sam. I need to do something about the damage to that relationship too, she's saying. And she's right. "I'll talk to him soon."

"Good." She leans in and kisses me softly. "But really, I'm here right now because of everyone I've ever met, you are the one person I can never stop thinking about. And it's starting to feel like maybe I'm that person for you."

"You are. And you were, before. Once upon a time. I promise you that I loved you then, so much. I've never stopped loving you. But then thinking about you got hard. I started to feel small and stupid. And I hid. I'll never hide again."

"Speaking of hiding…" She climbs off my lap and holds out her hand. "I want to show you something."

She leads me into her closet and pulls down one of the two vintage suitcases from her top shelf.

"Photos?"

She gives me an amused look. "Is that what you think is in here?"

I frown. "Isn't it?" I could have sworn she'd shown me some family pictures at some point. I hadn't paid enough attention, because I was a jackass.

Now I want to look at each one carefully. Inspect it for all the tiny clues I can gleam about who Grace is, where she came from. Every bit of her is exciting and fascinating, including the ancient history of baby photos.

She takes a deep breath. "No, these aren't photos. They're…" She turns pink. "Books. A collection, so to speak."

Cave of Sin
For Lust's Sake
The Sexiest Student
Spanking the Sitter
Their Secret, Younger Lover
The Wayward Daughter

I pick up the last one, and Grace turns red. "Some are more… No, actually, they're all pretty intense."

It doesn't take me long to figure out what she means. The words on the page are crude, violent, and obscenely out of date.

My wife collects misogynistic porn.

I don't really know what to make of that. I look up at her and smile, because this changes nothing. Everything about her complicated, clever mind is amazing to me. Even something like this that I'd never have expected and don't really understand. "Huh," I finally say.

She laughs.

"How long have you been collecting these?"

"Forever. I found my first one in college."

I think about all the times we've crawled through used bookstores on our travels. "Have you ever bought one in front of me?"

She nods, her lips pressed together and her eyes bright.

"Which ones?"

She points to *The Sexiest Student* and *Their Secret, Younger Lover*. "On our trip to London last year. At the used bookstore."

"I don't remember." There's so much about the last three years that are a fog to me.

"You bought a biography of Winston Churchill." She tips her head to the side. "And then we went to a pub, and you asked me what I bought, but I changed the subject."

Nothing. "Was that the same day we went on the Eye?"

"The day after that. You'd had meetings that morning, remember?"

I swear under my breath. "No."

"It's okay." She gives me a small smile that says *no, it isn't,* but that's Grace. Endlessly forgiving of the mess I've made of my life. Our life.

"I want to remember," I say hoarsely. "Tell me more."

"I dragged you to the Notting Hill market first. We paid too much for a print of a painting..." She cranes her neck, looking at the top of the closet on my side. "It's up there, I think."

I follow her gaze and see an edge of plastic at the top of the shelf. I reach up and grab it.

There are actually two prints there, and she gasps when she sees the other one.

I don't recognize it. But I do remember the one from London. "This...I remember you wanted this, and I..." I trail off. She'd wanted it, and I'd said it was ugly. She'd pouted and I'd given in, but I'd hurt her feelings. "I was rude."

She nods. Her eyes are wet, welling with tears, and I feel

impotent—a real, brutal, deep-down sense of not being enough. It's a million times worse than my dick being lazy sometimes.

"Let's frame it," I say gently. "Please. I want to. I remember that morning. My meetings. The coffee we got before we walked through the market. That was a great morning."

"It was," she whispers. "Until that conversation about the painting. I bought it anyway, out of spite, but then you checked out. And you don't remember the rest of the day, which—" She drags in a ragged breath. "Well, I guess I understand that now. But I don't like it, you know?"

"Yeah."

She gives me a grim smile and packs her books away.

I look at the other print. It's a coast at sunset. Similar colours to the English painting, but wilder. "What is this from?"

"I bought that for you on my work trip to San Francisco." She sighs and stands up, pushing past me. "I gave it to you when I got back. I'm pretty sure you don't remember that, either."

I don't.

I'm starting to realize there's a lot from the last three years that I don't remember, and that's really disturbing.

I can't stand what I *do* remember. What the fuck is going to happen when I realize just how truly awful I've been to the most important person in my entire world?

"We'll figure it out together." She brushes her fingertips over my mouth, and I realize I asked that question out loud. "I think it's time you come home."

27

GRACE

THAT NIGHT, he doesn't leave. We don't fool around, he just holds me as we fall asleep, and it's wonderful.

When I left Javi's hotel room, I was sure I just wasn't ready to have sex again, period, and there's still a part of me that thinks that might be true. I think that I hate how much I love the touch of Luke's skin against mine. How right that feels even after all the damage.

But the next day, I stop at a drugstore just in case and get a box of condoms. I tuck them into my underwear drawer, and there they sit, a ticking time bomb of dirty potential.

We make fresh spring rolls together for dinner, and it's just as flirty as the night before.

After dinner, as we're tidying the kitchen, I tap his hip to nudge him out of the way, and get a little too much front-of-the-jeans territory to be a polite nudge.

Luke groans as my fingers graze the half-ready bulge behind his jeans.

"Do you like that?"

He gasps as I grope him again. His gaze darkens as he backs me up against the counter, but only enough to cage me in. He doesn't take control, and I keep touching him. Tracing the shape of his cock, hard and long behind his fly.

"I like the sounds you make." I lick my lips. "You're never loud, unless you're trying to…"

His mouth twists. "Dirty talk?"

"Sometimes it was good. It was very good that time in your apartment downstairs…"

He tips his head to the ceiling, baring his neck, and I hop up onto the counter so I can pull him closer.

I hook my fingers into his waistband and tug.

He *groans*. Out loud, lusty and raw.

The tip of my middle finger is almost grazing him inside his jeans. Almost, but not quite. I tug him again, bringing him into the vee of my legs, and he shudders.

"Really?" I whisper against his neck, my lips brushing his tense flesh. "Is that hot?"

"My little bird being handsy and demanding? Her sweet little fingers almost brushing my cock?"

That right there. That's the good kind of dirty talk that I like. It gets under my skin because it's real, uncensored, just the like the noises he's making.

It's all authentic. Not an act, not a controlled version of what Luke thinks he should be.

This is who my husband *is*, and I'm only just seeing it now. "Little bird, eh?"

"Do you like that?"

I nod. And then I feel the siren call of the condoms. "Hey, can I ask you a question?"

He grins. "Of course."

I shake my head. This isn't quite right. I soften my voice. "It's a question for a Daddy."

His face firms up. "Oh?"

That shouldn't make my panties wet, but it does. Oh, it does. "Um, so...I need to demonstrate something for class."

"Timeout." He puts his hands in the air.

I laugh, my voice returning to normal. "Too much?"

"Nope, not at all. That was hot as fuck, and I think I like where this is going, but you said we needed to negotiate this stuff because you have some limits, and I think I need us to do that right now, before I ruin what might be the hottest thing ever."

My mouth drops open. "Oh. Yeah. That's...smart." I squirm on the spot. "All right. But you need to go first. Any limits?"

"I don't think so? I don't want you to tie me up." He gives me a helpless look. "Do I need to take that quiz right now? How long does it take?"

"Not long, but no. You can take it later. Right now, I guess just what I need you to know is that I'm going to say some stuff that makes me sound young, but that's a variable head-space state for me. It comes and it goes, and I'm always Grace. When we did this before, and you used my name...that was really hot." I take a deep breath. "I love our size difference, so if you call me little, I love that, and I like being baby girl, but I don't like any specific references to me being a child or anything like that."

He nods. "Totally. Down with all of that. But the school thing…?"

"Yeah. That's my headspace stuff. So think of it like an alternate dimension, where I'm me, Grace, a grown-up, but I also go to high school. I'm not a teenager, but… maybe innocent like one." His eyes do something very hot when I say innocent. There's a small tug in my belly that reminds me that he once chose a younger woman, but I can look at that and move on, because I like the rest of this. "Is that a good thing for you? The innocent stuff?"

"It is if it's you," he breathes, and sweeps me into his arms. "Very good thing. Very hot."

"Can we drop out of timeout? Because I have this assignment thing that I need help with…"

"Fuck yes." He plants a searing kiss on my mouth and lifts me up. "Where can I help you with this?"

"Bedroom."

He carries me to our room and sets me down.

I twist my arms in front of me and look bashful—except for my nipples, which are so hard I'm pretty sure they're giving away the plot a bit, but that's fine. It's supposed to be fun. This is everything I thought it could be and more. "So the thing is, for health class, I've been assigned a demonstration task, and I don't know how to do it."

His stern Daddy look is back. "Can you be more specific?"

I lean in close and whisper, "It's embrarassing."

He raises an eyebrow. *How can you demonstrate something if you're embarrassed by it?*

I know, right? Exactly why I need the help. "I'd rather show you, if that's okay."

"Of course." He glances at the bed. "Can I sit down for this?"

"Mm-hmm." I scurry to the dresser and open the box inside the drawer, drawing out just one condom wrapper. I turn around, keeping it behind my back, and join him on the bed.

I sit right beside him. Close enough that in a second, I can pull my hand from behind my back and set it on his thigh.

"Grace," he says, his voice low and private. "If you have something you need help with, you can always ask me anything. I'm happy to show you anything you might want to know."

"Really?" I look up at him and smile. "Do you mean that?"

A faint smile pulls at the corners of his mouth. "Yes."

I lean in and kiss him. Innocently.

He groans.

"Thank you," I whisper against his mouth.

Then I climb off the bed and stand in front of him, between his legs. He leans back, bracing himself on his hands, which is perfect.

"I need to know how to put on a condom," I say in a rush, pulling it from behind my back. I hold it out to show him, then drop my gaze to his erection. "And you're the only one I can think of to ask."

"Grace," he rumbles. "Are you sure about this?"

"Yes. I've seen it before, you know. In the shower. It's okay. It's just scientific."

That smile is back. "Is it, though? Are you sure you aren't being curious?"

"I promise."

He thinks about it for a second, then shrugs. "Okay. Go get a cucumber."

"No!" My protest is real, and so is the laugh he lets out.

He grabs me and hauls me onto the bed, tickling my sides. "Are you sure you aren't also a little curious about what Daddy's cock looks like?"

I squeak. "Okay, yes, maybe that."

"That's okay, Grace. Just be honest with me next time."

He kisses me softly, not quite so innocently this time, and I dart my tongue out to meet his as it licks my lower lip.

"That's not scientific," he whispers.

"But it is very curious, right?"

"Very." He kisses me again, deeper this time, and the condom drops out of my hand.

He picks it up, then rolls off the bed. "All right, let's get back to your assignment. When you take the condom out of the wrapper, you want to hold it like this, so it will unroll..." He demonstrates by rolling it a little bit down two fingers. "Like that. If it's flipped the other way, it won't unroll. That's the most common user error."

"Can I try?"

"Sure." He hands over the condom, and looks expectantly at my fingers.

I blush. "I meant can I try on your...cock."

He closes the gap between us and exhales as he hugs me to his body. I wrap my arms around him first, then slowly slide my fingers along his waistband, remembering how much he liked it when I tugged on his belt in the kitchen. "Please?"

I lean back, and the unexpected movement pulls him back onto the bed. As he tumbles, I scramble up him and get his belt undone.

He's breathing hard, letting me go. Pretending I'm doing it without permission, maybe.

I press up against him as my hand slides into his boxers. "Oh, you're so hard," I breathe. "Is that because I was talking about putting a condom on you?"

"Yes," he hisses. "Fuck."

"It's okay. You said this was our little secret, remember? You said I could rub against you any time I wanted."

"I meant with our clothes on," he groans. "Not like this. If you put a condom on me, Grace, I'm going to want to fuck you."

"Will you?" I gasp. "Will you fuck me? Will you use your big Daddy cock to show me what it feels like to be fucked with a condom on?"

"For science?"

"No," I whisper. "Just for me. This has made me all hot and achy. Like I need some kind of release."

"I bet it has. Me, too." He his hand around mine and squeezes, his erection throbbing in our shared grip. Then he crawls on top of me, bracketing my body with his. "Me, Luke. I want you, Grace."

I pull him down on top of me. I want his cock inside my body. I want to feel how hard he is for me.

It's been too long.

That's mine.

He pulls my clothes off as I find the condom, now abandoned and covered in lint. Swearing, he hops off the bed and goes to my dresser. "You have more in here?"

I nod.

He's back in a flash, his own clothes flying off at a remarkable rate.

And then he's on top of me, sheathed and ready. I lift my hips, eager for him, more than ready, even though I wasn't sure.

But I am now. I need him.

He rocks just the head in, taking his time. I stretch around him, crying out, and he makes the most beautiful sounds. *It's okay, you can take it, it won't hurt for long.* Horny, fictional lines that make me gush.

He pumps his cock into me in short, jerky thrusts. Just the tip, throbbing and pulsing as he comes. I imagine the hot spurts filling me up and my pussy flutters, already primed.

"God, Luke, just fucking do it, I need you." I claw at him. "Fuck me hard, fuck me so deep."

"I'm going to—"

"I don't care."

"Grace—"

"I'm there, too. Come with me. Deep. Fill me up."

He shudders as he thrust all the way in, restraint evaporating as I begin to clench around him. I've never come this fast before. It's a freight train of need, and now I'm shaking, the orgasm rioting through me as he bucks his hips. His left hand clenches in my hair as his right blindly grabs my calf, then my ankle, bending my leg up and open.

His fingers tighten around my ankle as he shouts my name again.

I close my eyes and sink into it, floating in the pleasure of my husband reclaiming my body. Finally. Yes.

Grace.

Yes.

28

LUKE

I'M STARTING to think I might never return to the office, and I don't mind that idea at all. I've gotten used to working from home. Grace and I can have leisurely mornings together, and then when she goes to the studio, I'm able to think about the big picture finance decisions without constant interruptions.

I know why Sam likes it so much now.

But it also raises the question of whether or not we're still the right people to lead this firm. Just because we founded it doesn't mean we need to stay there forever. Maybe I just want to be an angel investor for the rest of my career.

There's certainly enough money in that, and it would give me more time to devote to Grace.

I spend a lot of time thinking about our relationship as a long-term project. Trips I'd like us to take together, hobbies we might take up.

"How do you feel about tai chi?" I ask her as I browse the YMCA's website one evening.

"Who are you and what have you done with my husband?" she asks with a laugh.

"Who, that guy? What does Taylor Swift say? He can't come to the phone?"

She giggles. "You truly are a different person. But no, I don't think super slow is my preferred speed. What are you looking at?"

"The community classes at the Y. They seem…wholesome. I dunno. Just an idea." I hand her my laptop. "You have a look, see what you think."

She clicks on adult karate classes first, then the masters level swim club. "They have an information night next week, I think we could go to that. Let me check my calendar."

She opens a new browser tab and types in a webmail address. But instead of it going to a login page, it opens an email account I haven't looked at it in months.

That I had every intention of deleting.

Her face goes ashen. "Luke, what is this?"

"That's nothing." I want to throw up.

It's the burner email address I used to communicate with Caitlyn. There's nothing in the inbox, but she's smarter than that. She clicks on the sent folder and finds the last email I wrote. "You emailed her the day after I found out about the affair."

"And then I blocked her. You can see for yourself, she hasn't replied to it."

"You said just a few weeks ago that you had no more contact with her."

"I, I had no more contact with her. I didn't."

"But you emailed her. Here I can see it in this email account that I'm looking at right now that you left logged in on your laptop."

"That's not contact with her! I didn't speak to her." My heart is pounding as I desperately try to fix this. "She called and left a message for me at work, the morning after you found out. When I went into the office, Cameron gave me a message that she had called my office, and that was unacceptable. So I sent her that email—that single email—and then I blocked her. She can't respond to that message and you can see, there is no response."

"But you lied to me, Luke. I asked you if you had *any* contact."

"I didn't have any contact with her."

Grace jumps up. "You emailed her. And more to the point, you should have told me she called you. You don't get to keep secrets from me, even if you don't think they're secrets. I need you to be transparent with me on my terms, using the meaning of words as I understand them. Not your convenient-for-you definitions. I don't think we are at a place where you can be that callous or thoughtless about how I might feel."

"That was months ago. I haven't had any contact with her since that point. My phone is yours to look at, my computer is yours to prowl through. You're mad at me right now about something I did in the past. That's fine. But I'm not doing it now, so you're mad at Past Luke, not Present Luke. I'll do my best not to get defensive, but—"

She cuts me off. "But it's not you who I'm mad at?"

"Exactly!" I stand, too. "Do you want to take a shot at me?"

"No." She pauses. "No, I guess I don't."

"What can we do right now to reinforce what we have right now?"

She looks small and vulnerable and sad. "I don't know."

"Can we start with a hug?"

She paces away from me. "I need a minute. I just need to…" She lets out a rough breath and turns away from me.

I try not to panic, but it's hard.

Then I hear her counting to ten, and my heart breaks. That was fucking stupid, an unforced error, and she's right. I should have been more upfront about that bit of contact.

I tentatively move closer, and she sways, as if she wants to lean back against me.

And for what feels like the thousandth time, I whisper an apology to my wife.

29

GRACE

THE NEXT WEEK, we start couples counselling. Our therapist is someone Luke's counsellor recommended. She begins by using his favourite word.

"When we talk about repairing a relationship after an affair, it's important that we don't focus on the affair itself at first. That's an issue that isn't going to be solved, per se, because there's no changing the past. Repair is more about focusing on the future, and finding a softness, a peace in which you can move forward."

I nod along. I agree with all of that in principle.

"So this means we need to be able to have moments, like what happened last week, and learn to just sit with them."

"That stillness thing again," Luke mutters to me.

I smile at him, then explain the reference to the therapist.

She nods. "Can you sit with that pain now? Can you look at it without having a big reaction?"

"Yes." As long as I don't need to do anything about it. Pretend it doesn't exist.

She looks at me.

I stare right back. That's all she's getting. Yes, I can sit with it. I'm not giving her anything else to dig into right now. It's Luke's turn, and this is going to be hard enough as it is on him.

We both turn at the same time to give him our attention.

He's coiled tight. "Yeah," he says stiffly. "I can sit with it."

"It's okay," I say quietly, almost under my breath. "I know it's hard for you."

His jaw flexes. "I'll do whatever it takes." He swallows. "I hate what I did. I hate why I did it. I don't like to look at it."

Panic rises inside me and I breathe deeply, trying to stay in the moment. Just sit with it. Just look at. Don't react.

It's harder than it fucking sounds, that's for damn sure.

"Now I want you to both focus on this moment. And if I were to ask you to make a decision, a micro decision, what would your next move be? What would you do to shift yourself, in the smallest of ways, out of this pain."

"I don't understand," I say. "I'm not ready to get over it."

"I hear that. That's okay. I'm talking about micro moves. Imagine there's a string dangling in front of you, leading you out of this pain. Where does it go? If you take hold of it and take the tiniest of steps, what happens? Do you move towards Luke? Away from him?"

"Do I need to move?"

She purses her lips for a moment. "Can you tell me more about that?"

"I don't know what I want to do."

"You can choose to stay where you are. Are you holding the thread?"

I shrug. "Sure."

Luke leans forward. "I'll move towards Grace."

She nods. "Okay. Then do that."

I give her an alarmed look. "What?"

She smiles. "A micro move. Luke, shift your chair a centimetre towards Grace. No more. Just the tiniest of shifts."

He nudges his chair infinitesimally closer to mine.

"And now let's sit with this for a moment. Find that stillness."

Even though Luke and I have an in-joke about sitting still being scary, this is genuinely intense for me in a way I didn't see coming. Maybe because it's not just the two of us. For all our problems, we are a unit, and we see each other in every way. This therapist is a stranger. A professional, sure, but a stranger all the same.

And I'm letting her see that I struggle with giving my husband even an inch after what he's done. I'm not being defensive about that, I'm just being in my true essence.

Grace Preston, tired bitch.

"Now, if I were to ask you again…"

We repeat the exercise a few times, Luke moving closer to me by fractions of an inch each time, me not moving at all, feeling more and more settled and at peace with my decision to just hold on to the thread.

And then, on the fifth time, when she asks if I'm willing to make a micromove, I surprise all of us by saying yes.

Both of us move our chairs together a little tiny bit.

Then the therapist gets out a ruler, measures the distance between our chairs, and tells us we're out of time.

"That was weird, right?" Luke asks me as he holds the passenger side door open for me.

"Yeah."

"But a little good, too?"

I push up on my toes and kiss his jaw. "Yep."

30

LUKE

THAT NIGHT, we sit down and I finally take Grace's BDSM personality type quiz. Neither of us are surprised to find out that I'm as much a Daddy or caregiver as she is a Little or Middle.

And for the first time, we talk about safewords. We're going to start with just using stop and ouch, because Grace doesn't think she'll ever want to say stop and not mean it.

I'm fascinated by the layers there.

"So this class that you took," I ask her as she gets ready for bed. "This was at the kink club that Alex goes to sometimes?"

"Yep."

"And he knows about it?"

"The class? Or me taking it."

"That part."

"No, I don't think he does."

I rub my jaw. "I think I prefer it that way, if I'm allowed to have a preference."

She looks at me sideways. "You're allowed. One of the things I learned about caregiver kink is that it's often quite private."

"I can imagine."

"Speaking of that club..." She presses her lips together, then picks up her hairbrush. "Your brother might go there with Hazel."

I can feel storm clouds gathering in my head, and I'm not sure why exactly. It's a possessive thing, for sure. "Did you see him there?"

"Oh, no. He's a Preston, he would have combusted on the spot. But I found the card at his apartment, and that was bad enough." She hands me the hairbrush. "Would you brush my hair, Daddy?"

The storm clouds immediately recede. "Of course."

I watch her in the mirror as I centre myself, then I turn my attention to her hair. There are a few glints of silver at the crown. In a week, she'll have them covered up again with dye. She's fastidious about that, and only that, and I realize it's something we've never talked about.

I'm not about to tell her that I love her grey hair. Not yet. But I do, and I'll find a way to bring it up when she's not mad at me.

"Well go on," she whispers. "Brush my hair."

"Is there a..." I wrap my fingers around a section of hair, holding it so the brush doesn't tug her scalp. It goes through the strands like a knife through butter, so I relax and release the locks, and do it again.

She makes a pleased sound as the bristles make contact with her scalp. "That feels good."

"For me, too." I carefully pick another section of hair. "So if I wanted to learn more about how to do this, without running into my brother or my best friend..."

I get a smile in the mirror for that. "We can figure it out together. And there's a lot of good reading online."

"Is there? Bedtime story reading?"

"That, too." Her lips quirk. "Also more scientific stuff, if you wanted to assign me a book report or something like that."

"I like that idea."

She straightens her spine, her eyes flashing, and now it's all Grace. "Hey, speaking of Alex. I know he's been handling some of your work for a while now. Have you thought about going back to the office?"

"I've been thinking more and more about maybe not. We could sell the condo. Move out of the city. Explore subsistence living and non-stop orgasms."

"Lumberjack life?"

"You want me to chop wood for you without a shirt on?"

"Yes." She gazes at me with such soft longing it makes me desperate.

Again.

I crowd her against me, holding her tight with my arms, and press my mouth against her neck.

Her breath hitches as I graze her skin with my teeth. "Ah..." She gasps as I bite harder, an urgent whine that sends blood pumping to my dick. *Fuck, that's so filthy.*

"Remember your words," I growl.

Then I pick her up and carry her to our bed.

"I know..." she promises.

"Stop, or ouch."

"I didn't say any of them," she whispers.

No, but I'm never going to stop reminding she has outs if she wants them. That I'll only hurt her as much as she wants, only give her the pain she desperately craves.

"Good. Daddy likes how you put up with his hunger for your skin."

"Oh..." She writhes in the tight vice of my arms. "No, please..."

"Please mark you? Please sink my teeth into your flesh so you'll remember this when we can't be alone?"

She whimpers again. I haul her on top of me, my hands hard against her forearms. She's light as a feather as I manhandle her, pliant and perfect.

"Is that what you want, you little slut?" I hold her above me, arms pinned against her side, and use my mouth to rip her negligee down her torso, baring her breasts. "God, Grace. Your breasts are perfect."

She cries out for real as I latch on to one nipple. Her flesh is hot and swollen in my mouth, and I forget I'm supposed to be biting her because all I want to do is suck and lick and consume her in the softest way.

As her legs fold up on either side of me, her bare slit brushes against my belly, slick and soft, and I groan at the contact.

I shove my boxers down, low on my hips, bringing my

cock out to play. She gasps when it makes contact with the sweet, lush curve of her bottom, and I grind us together.

Then I flip us over and loom big above her.

She's soft beneath me, her arms stretched wide like she's floating on water. I touch her reverently, carefully, just my fingertips to start. Then my whole hand, wanting more contact with her skin. Lust churns inside me, but there's another clawing feeling competing to direct what I do next.

Adoration.

There is a laundry list of feelings I didn't allow myself to properly feel for my wife in the past, and lust has been top of that list most often. Showing Grace how much I want her has been my mission for weeks.

Tonight is different. And I'm honestly surprised at how this feeling dominates the lust. Yes, I want to fuck her. Yes, I want to be buried inside her. Yes, I want her scent imprinted on me, again. Yes, yes, always yes.

But that's about me.

I've let myself run wild with that because she needed to see it.

But she needs more than just that, too.

She needs to be adored, worshiped, honoured.

"Daddy loves you so much. Wants to keep you safe. Do you feel safe, little bird?"

She beams at me and nods. "And do you want Daddy to make you feel good?"

Another nod.

"Maybe a bedtime kiss, mmm?"

Her lips part, her eyelids fluttering half shut, and I give her a long, sweet kiss there, on her mouth, but that's not what I mean.

I crawl down her body, kissing each precious bit of her good night.

"Good night, Grace," I whisper against her neck. "Good night to your sweet, lovely breasts." She giggles as I lave her nipples, sucking the puffy points into my mouth. "Good night to your sweet belly, and this adorable little belly button, and the sweetest of good nights to your perfect pink pussy."

She gasps as I press her thighs apart and settle in, flat on the bed, for a very long, very filthy devouring of my wife's cunt.

She tastes perfect, musky and hot, and her flesh is already blooming for me as I lick between her folds, then suck her clit.

"Daddy can't wait to fuck this little pink hole," I growl. "One day soon, I might even go without a condom. Wouldn't that be nice, baby? Feel me inside you? Bare? Just you and me, nothing in between us?"

"Would you come inside me?" she asks in her dreamlike, fantasy voice.

"Deep inside you." I lap at the arousal spilling from her now. She likes that idea, and fucking hell, so do I. "Fill you with seed."

She cries out and tangles her fingers in my hair, pulling my mouth fully against her clit, and I suck her through her orgasm.

Then I sheath myself and thrust home, fucking her with

abandon. She comes again, clutching at me, and I growl in her ear one more time.

"Just like this. This is how I'll do it. Fill you all the way up with Daddy's seed."

"Fuck, Luke, yes…" She gasps and I lose it, my hips jerking out of control as my climax darkens the edges of my vision.

And then she laughs. "Wow. I mean, wow. Right? That was super dirty."

I nod and roll onto my back, my heart pounding.

31

GRACE

SPRING TURNS to summer far too quickly. I'm not sure if I like it. It's a reminder of time passing, of healing being slow.

Luke, on the other hand, likes the longer days. He's unhurried in the morning, and making dinner together stretches longer into the night.

When he approached Sam about hiring a new executive team for the firm, and stepping back into just being founders and investors, Sam was more on board with that idea than Luke thought.

And suddenly, my husband became a house husband of a sort.

So I shouldn't have been surprised when he brought up the topic of babies, but I was. It had been a long time since we'd discussed it in our twenties, and agreed then that we weren't interested in being young parents. Or maybe even parents at all.

"Why didn't we ever have kids?" he asks, clearly not having

the same memory of it that I do. We're sitting on the terrace having brunch.

"Because you were an asshole," I say lightly. "And things got rough there for a while."

An understatement.

"Did you want babies? Did I keep that from you?"

"No," I say honestly. "I wanted to make art."

"Is that still the case?" There's something about the way he says it, something searching and loaded, that I put down my espresso cup and give him my full attention.

"Why are you asking? Do *you* want kids?"

"I didn't before. Now…"

"Then it's the trauma speaking."

"I'm not saying I do right now." He shrugs. "And if you still don't, then it's a moot point. I want you."

But if I wanted a baby… Conversations like this can't be had in half-measure, with things left unsaid. Except I don't want him to say the rest of it. Not now. "If you still feel the same way in six months, bring it up again."

The corner of his mouth quirks, a tiny almost smile. "I will."

But I think about the conversation for days afterward.

It's one thing for me to decide to stay with him and renew our relationship despite the transgression. It would be another thing entirely to start a family with him. Can I be sure of his fidelity forever?

I'm shocked to realize that yes, I think I could be.

Only time will tell if that remains true.

And then there's the outstanding question of whether I gave moving on enough of an attempt.

Would I be happier if I left? Hypothetically, yes. I can see that path.

He betrayed me. But he's also dug deep and created a safe space for me to be real. Warts and all. Would I find that with someone else?

Maybe.

Another hypothetical.

I don't know which path holds more happiness. *That's* the truth. But I do know that this path is currently beautiful, full of happiness every day. That's messy and complicated, but it feels much more tangible than the hypothetical.

He's built me a path to happiness. The first few paving stones were fucking jagged. I never want to go back over them. But going forward? I believe him when he says it's going to just get better. That when I'm sixty, I'll look back and see two horrible, fucked-up years followed by twenty-five years of raw, unadulterated love.

Will it be worth the pain?

Only time will tell.

And I'm not ready to bring a baby into this family. Not yet.

It's funny how thoughts twirl through our minds, morphing. It's not like there was a direct line to whether or not I want babies—mid August, and the jury is still out on that—to me revisiting all the in-hindsight ways I was secretly kinky in my teens and twenties.

But looking back, I can remember individual purchases so clearly. And somewhere in storage, I remember with a start, I have a *Daddy's Girl* t-shirt I bought at a music festival a decade ago.

When I'm down there, I find it readily, but then I start picking through Luke's stuff, looking for any evidence of his relationship with Caitlyn.

I don't find any, and I'm left with a sick, angry feeling in the pit of my stomach. Lizard brain reaction, my own counsellor would say. I'm two months into therapy, and I thought I was getting past those worries.

I can't keep digging, can't keep picking at this scab. Not if I want to stay with him. Not if I want to be happy.

I grab the t-shirt and run all the way up eight flights of stairs, bursting into our loft with a gasp.

He looks at me, setting down the book he'd been reading. Instantly, I know I have his full attention. "What do you need?"

Big, intense feelings well up inside me. I could cry right now. I could puke. I'm definitely shaking, because how long have I wanted this, how long have I wanted his gaze on me, his undivided attention and concern?

And now I have it, at considerable cost.

This is a brutal kind of beautiful. I clench my hands tight at my sides. I don't cry. I don't puke. I lift my chin. "I'm overwhelmed. Can you crowd out the bad feelings?"

"I can do that, baby. Put your head in Daddy's lap."

I scramble across the room and drop to my knees, pressing my face into his lap. I don't understand why this feels so good, why it calms the storm inside me.

He combs his fingers through my hair, then rubs my neck. When I'm calm, I look up.

He's smiling at me.

"I found something in the basement that I want to wear for you."

"I want to see it."

I blush as I hold it up, and he helps me stand. I pull off my shirt, and my bra, because this new shirt is definitely meant to be worn bare chested.

I tug the t-shirt down over my breasts, the cotton rubbing against my nipple. Holding on to the hem, I stretch the fabric in vain. There's no way it'll cover my belly button.

"It's a little small," I whisper, heat blooming in my cheeks. "But I like it."

"I like it too." Luke's voice grates rough in the air between us and I jerk my head up. His eyes are dark and glittery. "So much. Come sit in my lap, baby girl. Show Daddy your shirt. I don't think it's too small."

"No?" I crawl toward him. As soon as I'm within grabbing range, his hands are on me and I'm tumbling against him.

He's got a condom in his pocket, because we're fucking all the time now, and he has it on and is buried inside me before I'm all the way ready.

This is my filthiest, favouritest way to have sex.

Daddy needing me and making himself fit inside me when I'm too tight.

It's fast and desperate and I start to whine, so I grab his hand and press it hard against my mouth.

Eyes wide, he clamps down, silencing me.

I come immediately.

He follows right after.

I sprawl in his lap once we're disentangled, feeling silly and light and perfect. "That wasn't too much?"

"No. That was hot." He drags in a ragged breath. "Honestly, Grace, I don't think you can go too far. If you want it, if it makes you hot, I'm in. Whatever you want. Whatever I can give you. Even if it's not something that I'd have imagined before, if it gives you that gleam in your eye…it's good."

"Okay."

"I'm surprised you haven't bought little white panties yet," he says with a chuckle, his lips rubbing against my temple.

No, I couldn't. It would be too much. Too on the nose.

Too dirty.

FIVE HOURS LATER, I find myself standing in Walmart, figuring out what four-pack of white panties I should buy—if I can bring myself to do it, because I feel *filthy*.

Hot, uncomfortable flashes of desire zap through me. Luke's fingers tracing the edges of the cotton, snapping the elastic.

Sliding underneath and groaning when he finds me wet and slick.

Whispered confessions of want. Begging pleas for more. *No, we can't. Nobody will know. Please, Daddy.*

Yeah, they shouldn't sell these panties. They're obscene.

And I can't buy them. I'll spontaneously combust at the register. Plus if Luke is home when I get back—which he will be—and if he helps me unload the groceries—sure to do—then I'll die all over again when he picks up the underwear and knows what I've done.

So that's exactly why I do buy them.

A perfectly innocent pack of women's white panties.

I'm going to hell, but I'm going there happy.

32

LUKE

December

MY BROTHER IS SKIPPING Christmas this year.

Only fair. Last year, I was a jerk to him, and so he skipped Christmas and reconnected with the love of his life. This year, they're taking that same trip again.

But I miss him.

It's quite the surprise to me to realize that.

We have a tree this year. Grace is currently lying on top of me on the couch, and we're admiring our bang up decorating job.

She nestles her head under my chin and exhales, going soft. "Do you want to talk about it?"

"Talk about what?"

"Whatever is on your mind."

My first instinct is to say no, but there's something about the soft weight of her that makes me pause. Do I want to talk?

No, I'm not ready. Will I feel better if I share my burden with my spouse? Yes.

Why do I resist that so much? What am I afraid of?

"It's stupid," I mutter.

"Try me."

"I miss Sam."

"Oh, honey." She props her chin on her hands and gives me a sad smile. "I think deep down he misses you, too. But all the work you've done with me, you'll have to do with him, too."

"Yeah." I make a face.

She pokes me in the side and laughs.

"There's something else on my mind, too." I twirl a lock of her hair around my finger. "In the summer I asked you about kids."

She stills. Her spine straightens, and she lifts her chin, as if the conversation is replaying in her mind. "You did."

"You said I could bring it up again in six months."

She laughs, a frown pulling her eyebrows together. "Did you set a calendar reminder?"

I shake my head, no. "It just came to me. It's not urgent, but if you are willing to entertain the conversation, I'd like to talk about it."

She relaxes again and rests her head on my shoulder. "We'll always be a bit chaotic. That's probably not good for kids."

"Life is chaos, maybe we can teach them to survive it better than I was taught."

That trips a soft, soothing sound out of her.

Was that a dirty trick? I don't want to play games with her heart.

"And maybe we'd have two boys? Brothers? And we could teach them…"

She rises again, launching herself right up to my face. "Maybe," she says. "Ask me again in six…" Her eyes are sparkling. "No, seven days."

"A week?" That's New Year's Eve.

Alex's annual house party, which Sam will be attending.

"Hazel and I have something planned. Up to you if you want to use that opportunity to talk to your brother."

A WEEK LATER, Grace and I show up at Alex's place early, because she's bringing art with her. Two pieces, both wall-mounted. They're boxed up, and she's being mysterious about them, but I'm clear on the fact that this is part of the surprise she's worked on with Hazel.

But Sam and Hazel don't arrive until much later, and when they do come in, he's the one who looks reluctant.

I recognize that expression. That was me last year. And that was part of what is causing him this discomfort right now.

Grace swoops over to them, welcoming them both, and getting right to the point. Hazel nods, and then Alex—clearly in on it—turns down the music and gets everyone's attention before handing the floor to Hazel, explaining that he was thrilled to host an impromptu art moment.

Impromptu my ass.

"I'm going to be reading two poems for you. *From Broken to Whole* and *A Full Exploration of the Aftermath*. They are pieces I developed as part of a project with my dear friend, Grace Dunn, inspired by her very first art show."

Grace stepped forward. "Thank you to Alex for allowing us this brief indulgence. We're grateful for the opportunity to share with friends and family this intimate project, inspired as Hazel mentioned by a show I did in university called The Art/Lit Project. It was a joy to work collaboratively with Hazel on these pieces. My sculptures hang on Alex's wall behind Hazel. On the left is *From Broken to Whole*, and on the right is *A Full Exploration of the Aftermath*."

My heart pounds in my chest as Hazel reads her poems. They're beautiful and raw and vague enough they could be about anything. They're in keeping with the style of Grace's work in general, but I know what this really is.

It's an opening for two stubborn brothers to share a little something.

Fucking hell.

When they finish, Sam and I both approach them, because of course we're fucking proud. Of them. Not each other. Not anymore.

So I clap him on the shoulder, as we do, Preston style, and I jerk my head to the kitchen. "Let's grab a beer."

He clears his throat and follows. We each grab a bottle, then I head upstairs, looking for some quiet. I find it in a spare room.

"I owe you an apology—" I start, at the same time as he says, "Look, Grace really wants—"

He stops.

I start again.

"I've handled the firm stuff not that well, and it's because of some relationship stuff Grace and I have been going through. I think tonight's performance was their way of pushing us to talk."

"Hazel sort of nudged me in that direction, yeah." He frowns. "Is it addiction? Alex thought—we weren't gossiping, but—"

"No. Not really."

"It's okay, you know. Grace once told me that recovering from trauma means that you need to come to terms with the ways you coped with the pain."

A hot, searing pain slices across my chest. "This is different."

"Is it?"

I don't answer that.

And my silence speaks volumes—and maybe Sam has always seen that I am capable of the absolute worst.

His face pales. "You cheated on her."

"Yeah. It's done. In the past."

"Fuck you. I should—" He drags in a breath. "And Hazel knew?"

"I don't know what she knows. That's between her and Grace. They need some secrets, maybe. It's hard to be in love with Preston men."

Sam shakes his head. "I spent the last year waiting for

Grace to leave you because she had outgrown your relationship. And you're telling me she was working on repairing it?
In secret? To protect you? You don't deserve her."

"Of course I don't. But I'm damn glad she doesn't agree."

"And we're not fucking Preston men. Not really."

"Well, yeah. Sure. But in nature versus nurture, at least in
my case, nature didn't do me any favours."

"Mine either." Sam growls. "You know what? I was so mad
at you for so long. But it was really Dad."

"Me, too. But I turned into him. That's fair."

Sam makes a face. "Do you ever think about the fact that
we don't know who our real fathers are? For sure?"

"Nope." I grab him by the shoulder and squeeze. "It doesn't
matter. We have each other."

"Grace make you go therapy?"

"I go willingly."

"Took me a while."

"It's good, though, right?"

"Yeah."

"Luke?"

"Yeah?"

Sam stands and shoves his hands in his pockets. "I love
you."

Ah, fuck it. I haul him in for a tight hug. "I love you, too. So
fucking much."

"And if you ever hurt Grace again, I'll murder you in your
sleep."

"Never, brother. I promise you, that will never happen."

He claps me on the shoulder and we go back downstairs.

As soon as I hit the bottom of the landing, Grace's gaze is locked on my face. *All good,* I mouth.

I love you, she says back. And she says it with her whole body, lighting up.

I press my hand to my chest. *I love you, too, little bird.*

THE ART/LIT PROJECT

BY GRACE DUNN AND AIBHLIN MOON

Broken to Whole
by Aibhlin Moon

From broken to whole
Brittle to soft
This is her goal
His goal
And yet
The path between broken and whole
Is barbed
The journey from brittle to soft
Is treacherous
Soft is effort
Whole is precarious
So they must be careful
Together

A Full Exploration of the Aftermath
by Aibhlin Moon

A full exploration of the aftermath
Of an explosion
A fracture
A cut
Requires careful
Thorough
Relentless observation
And that painstaking process
Hurts

ALSO BY AINSLEY BOOTH

If you want more kinky, Canadian erotic romance...
Secrets and Lies
Tempt
Crave

Frisky Beavers
Prime Minister
Dr. Bad Boy
Full Mountie
Mr. Hat Trick
Page of Swords
Bull of the Woods

If you like intense, off-limits book boyfriends... **Forbidden
Bodyguards**
Hate F*@k
Booty Call
Dirty Love
Wicked Sin
Filthy Liar

If you like silly, sexy, over the top fairy tale romances...

AN EXCERPT FROM TEMPT

HAZEL

I'm the last to board the business class car at the front of the train. After carefully stowing my carry-on, I make my way down the car, looking for my seat. I should have a seat to myself. I always do.

Every trip, apparently, except this one. I silently groan as I realize I'm in a backwards-facing seat—fine—across from someone else.

Less fine. I don't want to share my table.

I see a dark head of hair. Masculine hair, as much as one can anticipate that sort of thing. The long leg and big arm overflowing the generous seat is a warning sign, too. Some slick businessman, it looks like, taking up far too much space in what was going to be my writing cocoon for the next four hours.

Well, I hope he likes silence, because I'm going to ignore the fuck out of him.

He doesn't look up as I move past and dump my messenger bag on my seat. Coat off, computer out.

And it's because I have that emotional armour up—I'm focused on ignoring my seatmate and getting my work done —that when I sit down, and his dark gaze locks on my face with a blazing intensity, I don't react.

We're strangers. I owe him nothing. In the spirit of the season, I flash a polite but dismissing smile and take my seat.

Headphones up and on. Plug in the cord. Open the computer.

I ignore the weird hiccup in my pulse. Ignore the man, and his searing gaze, which he's now thankfully dropped.

(Okay, I only know this because I looked up again. For a split-second. Curiosity will kill me as surely as it killed the cat.)

I'm not sure what I'm feeling right now. Deja vu, but not really. A weird disconnect because I'd filled in a generic proto-man as my seatmate when I saw the suit, the arm and leg taking up too much space, the roughly slicked-back, sharply side-parted haircut.

You noticed a lot about his hair. More than I'd realized, and something in my belly quivers.

His haircut doesn't matter.

His face, his gaze, that unsettling sizzle—none of it matters.

I open my files and give myself a goal. Three more revisions before the porter comes around with the first round of drinks. Then I can close this project and free-scrawl anything I want for my blog. Write drunk, edit sober—advice not meant to be taken literally, but it's never steered me wrong.

But the words on the screen swim in front of my eyes.

It takes a painfully long stretch of time to get into my task. Two glasses of red wine help with my concentration. Help to slow down my racing pulse and finally, thankfully, crystallize my attention.

An hour later my revisions are done. It's not the best work I've ever done, but it's entertaining and hot. Good enough. I fire the document off to my editor with a note that I'll be out of the office for the next four days and would be happy not to get it back for the final pass until after the new year.

Then I sneak a quick glance across the table. At *him*. He's still buried in his phone. His hair is ridiculous. He probably spends more on his cuts than I do mine.

His suit looks expensive. So do his shoes, his tie... I'd rather imagine him in jeans. Fitted ones that hug his thighs. A Henley with the sleeves rolled up, revealing his forearms. Corded, tan from time in the sun. A light dusting of dark hair that looks soft and feels softer.

I can't help it.

This is what I do. I see people and they turn into sex in my head. It was only in the last few years that I figured out I could actually do something with the super dirty vignettes that form unbidden in my mind.

Jeans, a rolled up shirt sleeve. That burning gaze—there's a lot to work with there.

No words, no explanations. Just a hot sex scene set to a dirty, thuddy beat.

We're in a dance club, yelling over the music, and then, when that proves frustrating, Mr. Searing Gaze takes me—no, not me—takes my character by the hand—no, the wrist, his fingers hot and firm as they manacle around her flesh—and leads her to a nook off a dark hallway.

I write and re-write, typing words quickly, then deleting some of them before madly dashing out more.

The dark hallway is still loud. Too loud to be heard, but that's not his goal. He wanted privacy, and now they have some.

He asks with his body—can he touch her? Should he kiss her?

Yes. No. Do it anyway. She leans in anyway and gives him her mouth, her legs, a grind of her sex. He finds her waist, then higher. Her breasts. Her nipples, and then—

The train slows to a halt. I lift my hands off the keyboard, the fantasy word blitz temporarily pausing.

I glance out the window, but there's nothing to be seen. No lights, no town. No stop was announced, and we're only an hour and a half outside of Toronto. Not quite to Kingston. Maybe we need to let another train pass before we can continue.

The perfect head of hair doesn't look up.

I take a deep breath and go back to the story, but without the white noise of the train rushing along the tracks, I can't do it. As if he could hear the filthy words I'm spinning on this side of my computer screen if it were too quiet in our little mini compartment.

Maybe I don't need to write anything else tonight anyway. I've got enough for a Christmas gimme to my blog followers. I'll polish this up when I get to the hotel, then post it before bed.

Then the train jerks backwards, and my computer skitters off the table between us, sliding precariously towards the aisle.

He catches it deftly, and I stand up, reaching for it. "Sorry." My heart pounds in my chest, because *oh God he's holding porn about himself*, but he doesn't know that.

"It's not your fault," he says, handing it over.

And then the train jerks again, forwards this time, and I tumble back into the leather seat, clutching my laptop to my chest.

He swears under his breath and looks around, then back to me. "Are you all right?"

"I'm fine." I peer out the window again, but it's pitch-black out there and bright in here. I can't see anything. "That was… sudden. Twice."

"Yeah." He looks me over, like he's sizing me up. Both for injuries—and I really am fine—and also for how to handle this new talking thing. I smile tightly and take off my headphones, which had fallen around my neck in the whole yanking forwards and back anyway. He taps on his phone screen, then rolls his neck with a groan. "There's been a collision up ahead on the tracks."

"How do you know?"

He turns the phone screen so I can see it. Twitter. "Hashtags."

I'm not sure why the train staff haven't said anything. "Maybe it's just a short interruption to service."

"Maybe."

I clutch my computer tighter.

"Are you sure you're okay?"

"Yep."

"Good. I—" He's interrupted by the intercom.

"Bon soir..." The announcement was read out in French first, which I don't speak, so I listened patiently until it repeated in English. *"Good evening, ladies and gentleman. We apologize for the sudden stop. We have a delay on the tracks ahead and have received instructions to hold position here for the moment."*

Damn it. He was right. "That's too bad," I say quietly, my heart sinking. Of course I hope whoever is in the collision is all right, and this could just be a short delay until they get the tracks cleared.

"I guess, uh..." He gives me a rueful smile, like he knows that I didn't want to talk, but now we're talking anyway, so the polite thing to do is do it right. "Can I introduce myself?"

My sinking heart jolts back into place. It's an odd request, but I like it. I smile. "Sure."

"I'm Sam. Sam Preston."

I nod. Okay. Let's do this. I hold out my hand. "I'm Aibhlin."

*

That's all he gets. My writing nom de plume, and only the first name at that. I don't give him my last name. I don't want him to google me with the same speed he found the news about the train stoppage.

"A pleasure, Aibhlin." He repeats it exactly right, his pronunciation perfect. *Aveline*. No weird reaction, no questions. His gaze doesn't leave my face, and his smile seems sincere.

I relax a bit. "Same to you, Sam."

Then I put my computer in my bag, because who am I kidding? I'll be too on edge to write any more words tonight.

And if we're going to do this, I'm going to do it right.

He gives me another smile. This one is bolder. Inviting, seductive. *Do you want to play a game? Flirt instead of work?*

I don't. Not really. I didn't, anyway.

I glance at his hand. No ring. Means nothing, but I'm jaded now. I always check. "Heading to Ottawa for work?"

He nods.

I pick up the stemless wine glass that holds the remnants of my second drink. "And what do you do, Sam Preston?"

The corner of his mouth pulls up, forming an almost-dimple right at the point. Does he like the full name treatment? "I'm an investment banker."

I can't help it. I laugh. "Of course."

He gestures down at his suit. "Predictable?"

"Entirely."

"And you?"

Before I can answer—and who am I kidding, I wasn't

going to anyway—the door between the train cars clatters open behind me.

I turn and look at the steward, who is pushing the drinks cart. Just in the nick of time.

"Sorry about that, folks. I was in the next car over and it took some time to get back. You heard the announcement? We're going to be here for a bit."

"What's the problem?" Sam asks, as if he doesn't already know from Twitter.

The attendant doesn't give us a real answer. "A delay on the tracks is all I've been told so far." He gestures to the cart. "Good thing we're well stocked. Can I get you another drink, miss? And then I'll be back with dinner service shortly."

Miss. My lips twitch and I hold out my glass. "Top me up. And keep calling me miss, I like that."

"Of course." He gives me a generous pour, then turns to Sam, who so far into this trip has declined service. "And you, sir?"

Sam exhales roughly. "Well, if we're going to be here for a while, I'll take a rye on the rocks. Make it a double."

That's more like what I expected. Investment banker. Make it a double. There's something reassuring there. I know what to do with a man like this. Play with him, have my fun. Under no circumstances will I trust him, but that's all right.

Trust is overrated.

Once we're alone again, Sam lifts his glass in a toast. "To comfort while we wait."

I drink to that. "I hope nobody is hurt too badly."

"Same." He takes a big swallow, his throat working quickly

to down the fiery alcohol. No hesitation. Then he gestures to the window, where it's started snowing. Big, fat, swirling flakes of white brush against the window. "Maybe the tweets are wrong. Maybe the train is stopped for another reason, like the weather."

I'd like that. No injuries, no accident that's ruined a family's night.

"A storm," I murmur, my imagination twisting the newly swirling snow into a monster. "Ice demons."

I love the look of surprise on Sam's face as his brows hit the roof. "Ice demons?"

"I like it better than an accident three days before Christmas."

He shrugs. "Fair enough. There you go. So they've whipped up a weather system right in front of us? Iced the tracks and now we can't move forward?"

"Something like that." I hadn't meant to say ice demons out loud.

But Sam is rolling with it. "Are they angry at the train for some reason, or are we caught in between a battle between foes?"

And because he's into the story, so am I. "They could be fighting over a woman on the train? Or maybe it's one ice demon, and his beloved is on here somewhere. She's the only one who knows why we've stopped. And she's…" I lick my lips, trying to get it just right. What would she be feeling?

"Torn?"

"Terrified," I correct him. "This is the end of their story, maybe, and it feels like a life-or-death flight on her part. Now he's stopped her, trapped all these people."

"She's scared of him?"

I shake my head. "No. But she's scared of what he makes her feel."

He smiles. "You're a romantic."

"Only on the page."

"Ah. Touché."

Sorry to disappoint, buddy. I live in the real world. "How about you?"

He rolls his shoulders back, flexing inside his three-thousand-dollar suit jacket. No, he doesn't like romance. The jacket, the wolfish smile, the practiced way of offering to buy a woman a drink just to pass the time by—this guy is just as jaded about people as I am. He knows what's what. "I like the idea of it," he finally says. "In theory. But I think there's a solid chance the big scary demon is, in fact, the bad guy. I guess I hope that it all works out in an unexpected way in the end. Maybe the romance is—" He cuts himself off.

I'm not sure what we're talking about anymore. What happened to dirty flirting?

He immediately looks sideways, releasing me. He's good. Knows just how far to push, then pulls back. He wants to keep this fun, and frankly, I'm grateful for that. We could be here for hours.

His gaze locks on something—nothing, but he's pretending—out in the darkness. Beyond the sleeting white stuff, past the tree line.

To our imaginary boogeyman. To the territorial hero,

stalking the train out of misguided but romantic affection for a heroine.

"What happens next?" he asks, his voice low enough that this is just for us. The other passengers can't hear it. "On the page. With this ice demon and his beloved, stuck on the train."

"She knows the ice demon is upset. And she's worried that he doesn't know the strength of his own abilities." I like the way Sam leans in as I start weaving the story. I don't want to like it too much, but there's something about the look in his eye that emboldens me. Like he'll like anything I say here, I can be as wild as I want with this fantasy tale. "Maybe he doesn't know that a storm can interfere with travel plans, cause car accidents, or down power lines."

And that's when the lights in our car flicker and go out.

I don't gasp. Other people do, further down the train car, and then I hear Sam chuckle.

"That was a neat trick," he says as he taps his phone, lighting up the space between us weakly. I refocus my eyes on his grin. "What next, storyteller?"

"The ice demon takes a nap and the lights came back on," I say under my breath, but no such luck. I take a sip of wine. "Our heroine realizes she needs to find a way to communicate with the ice demon."

"Whoa, hold up, we've got a major plot hole." Sam clears his throat. "With all due respect to the narrator. But how did they fall in love if they can't talk?"

"Well he's not always in the form of a giant ice demon conjuring a storm. When he's not upset, he's like…seven feet tall and built like a cross between an NFL and an NBA player. And whatever he touches turns a little bit cold. Like he makes you shiver with each stroke, every caress."

"Sexy," Sam deadpans. He lifts his glass and takes another big swallow of rye, then wipes his mouth. My eyes have adjusted to the dim light, the entire car dark except for electronic glows here and there. It's eerie and intimate at the same time.

But more importantly, Sam doesn't understand the appeal of a sexy ice demon. I re-focus my attention. "You haven't had enough fun with—"

He reaches across the table and touches my hand. Hidden under his fingers is an ice cube, and the cold press against my skin makes me shiver exactly as I just explained.

"Ice," I whisper, finishing my thought.

"Tell me more about him," Sam murmurs, his eyes carefully watching me. "He's a man?"

"Some of the time." I suck in a breath as he moves his touch up my hand and onto my wrist.

"More?" His fingers slide onto the inside of my arm and I turn my hand over.

Yes, more.

He continues asking questions like he's not molesting my skin with a melting ice cube. "And the rest of the time?"

"Uh, he's a storm. Well, a larger-than-life man-shaped demon surrounded by a storm. He needs to take that shape regularly, although he can be an only slightly larger-than-life man most of the time."

"What happens in the summer?"

"You and your plot holes." I swallow hard. "He's gone in the summer. He has to travel somewhere cold."

"Brutal."

The lights flicker, and in a flash, Sam's touch is gone. By the time the train car is fully lit again, he's leaning back in his seat, the quintessential picture of the unconcerned man. I blink, adjusting to the brightness, and it's almost like all of that didn't just happen.

"*Bon soir...*" The announcement apologies for the temporary power interruption in French first, and then English. "*A power cable unhooked between the cars. The problem has been repaired, and your dinner service will begin shortly.*"

"No ice demon," I say.

Sam almost smirks, but he reins it in at the last second. "Are you disappointed?"

I don't answer him. Instead, I drain my wine glass.

"Do you want another drink?" He twists around, looking for the attendant.

I take a deep breath. "Probably shouldn't."

He smiles again, a slow and dangerous grin. "Probably not."

A hot, needy tug pulls low in my belly.

His gaze slides down my body as if he knows what the wolfish smile does to me inside. Then he snaps his eyes back to my face. "Do you want to play it safe, *Aibhlin*?"

The inflection is more effective than a bucket of ice water on my libido. My back straightens, and I tighten my legs.

No more languid fun. This train can get moving any time now. We didn't even get to dinner. "Oh, Sam. Why did you have to go and say it like that? Our game was so lovely there for a hot second."

His face tightens up. "Is that what it was to you? Some kind of game?"

"Of course. And it was for you, too. Obviously, with your *'I'm Sam. Sam Preston,'* nonsense."

His eyes flick to the window, to the now more chaotic snow and the darkness beyond. When he looks back, his smile is more familiar. Rueful.

Boyish, like I remember it from ten years ago.

ABOUT THE AUTHOR

Ainsley Booth a three-time USA Today bestselling author of erotic romance. Between her two pen names (she also writes contemporary romance as two-time New York Times best-seller Zoe York), she has published more than fifty books since 2013. Notable hits include *Prime Minister* and *Hate F*@k*.

9 781989 703793